UNLIKELY PREY

Novel by
KATHE ARENDT

Acknowledgement

*Thank you, my dear friend, editor, and sage advisor…
without you, the book wouldn't have been completed*

CHAPTER ONE

The wheels of the private jet softly bumped and skidded across the tarmac at the small airport in Boca Raton, Florida. Karen quietly exhaled while James remained asleep in his seat as the plane taxied toward the terminal. The third passenger, Miguel Travares, was reading a Brazilian newspaper unfazed by the landing. Karen recalled what Miguel told her before they left his ranch in Brazil, "no one saw us, no one knows we were there, and we won't be tied to my cousins' disappearance." It was hard to digest what just happened over the past five weeks. Karen, a former FBI agent, knew it was unlikely they would get caught, but she was an active participant in a murder plot, and that was unsettling.

Miguel's cousin's, 34-year-old maniacal twins, killed James' only daughter Elizabeth Caulfield. The police never solved the case, the twins walked free, and that's when the trio hatched a plan to exact justice. While their plan was executed with precision, James paid a dear price. His emotions ran high and during an unplanned encounter, the twins broke free from their shackles and beat James so badly he almost died. Karen vowed to leave the events in Brazil in the past now that she was home. She wanted nothing more than a quiet peaceful life with her beloved James Caulfield III, that is, once she erased the vision of him in that hospital bed. She can't remember ever being so terrified.

The police investigation into Elizabeth's death ended rather quickly. Local law enforcement assumed it was a suicide death from a heroin overdose, and they closed the case. The three friends on the plane avenged her death for different reasons. Miguel felt responsible for her death because he introduced her to the killers at a party he hosted, and it gnawed at him. James loved her and knew his daughter wasn't drug user, nor would she ever take intentionally her own life. Karen loved James and in the short time she got to know Elizabeth, she also believed her death was a homicide. They each had motive to seek their own brand of justice. A few weeks after the police investigation was officially closed, Karen and James followed Miguel to Bahia Brazil after he located the twins. The plan was complete when the family yacht exploded with the twins aboard. The couple owed a debt of gratitude to Miguel because of his help and careful planning, the menaces who brutally murdered Elizabeth Caulfield were they out of their lives forever.

As the small jet came to a stop on the tarmac, Jill Freeman, Miguel's girlfriend, was inside terminal full of anticipation for his arrival. The couple was about to be reunited, and that sat well with Karen; after all, when her friends were happy, she was happy. It was as if time stopped for all of them after Elizabeth's death, and James was heartbroken over the loss of his daughter as any father would be.

Once off the plane, the foursome left the small airport in separate cars. Karen and James rode home with a driver in comfort. He put his arm around Karen and leaned his head back on the leather seat while she took in the familiar sights through the tinted windows. They were exhausted and that made for a quiet ride. The car pulled into the long driveway of the beach-house on a sunny April day; Karen opened the window and the fresh salty air tickled her nose. As they drove further up the driveway, the scent from the magnolia trees washed over her. The long driveway wrapped around the front of the house in a semi-circle smile and the lush landscape provided a warm green hug. While they sat in the chauffeured sedan, James held Karen tightly before they exited the car and whispered, "You're home." They had been through a lot together during their first year, and their feelings for each other had grown deeper because of it. Karen finally agreed to move in with him after being asked three times.

Once they dropped their bags in the entryway, they opened all the windows to let the fresh sea air in. Karen changed clothes, tossing on shorts and an oversized t-shirt. She encouraged James to take a nap since he still wasn't 100% after being in the hospital for almost two weeks. He had suffered a traumatic brain injury from the beating, and couldn't simply will himself back to good health without allowing time to heal. He had a number of doctor appointments to line-up now that they were back in the States and Karen intended on nursing him back to good health whether he wanted her to or not. It did her heart good to see him lying on top of the bed soundly asleep shortly after his head hit the pillow.

As he slept, she relaxed into the corner of the tan leather sectional in the living room. The faint sounds from the waves washing ashore echoed rhythmically in the background, and she wondered if a house could have a soul. The tri-level home was deceiving at first glance. From the street side, hidden behind greenery and lush plantings, it didn't appear to be 4600 square feet. However, once inside, with the sweeping views, the open floor plan, and the lower level built atop pillars on the sandy beach below, it felt bigger than it was. From the ocean side, it looked like a fortress. The mirrored glass provided privacy, and the steel frame construction was unshakable during the last hurricane. The muted tones of the interior décor peacefully coexisted with the magnificent views outside. The house felt like home since the first night she stayed there, and she melted into the scenery while she dreamt about their future together.

After a restful nap, James took a long hot shower, dressed, and joined her on the deck for a drink and a light snack. He stood at the rail and stared out at the ocean for a long while. Karen knew his silence meant his thoughts were with his daughter. He wanted to scatter her ashes in the ocean and Karen hoped he would wait until he was healed. However, knowing him as well as she did, the ceremony would probably take place sooner rather than later. He poured two glasses of wine and broke the silence.

"I'd like to have a special dinner on the beach this weekend and release Elizabeth's ashes into the sea. Once I get the scans on my head out of the way, I want to get back to our lives."

Since it was only Tuesday, Karen thought the weekend was a perfect choice. "I think it's a great idea and I'd like to cook a special meal for us."

He shook his head, "I'd rather have it catered, that way you can relax. We will honor her here because she loved this house and we've had a lot of memories on this beach. She was happy I met you and I want to celebrate our life together, as well as hers, and there's no better place for her ashes to be released than on this beach."

"Just let me know what time I should be ready."

CHAPTER TWO

They arrived at the Orlando office of Barron Neurological Institute at 11:00 am the next morning for James' CT scan of his head. The one-story building had parking in front, and they pulled into a visitor's space in plenty of time for the 11:30 apt. Once inside, an elderly receptionist with a volunteer badge welcomed James with warm smile while she confirmed his appointment time. The lobby was crowded, and they found two seats together next to a chubby woman with strongly scented perfume that smelled like vanilla. Karen worried that the long flight from Brazil aggravated his delicate condition and neither of them were confident the pressurized jet cabin didn't cause additional harm. The scan was necessary to make sure the swelling around his brain subsided.

It wasn't long before he was summoned back to the desk. He returned with six forms to complete and tapped his shirt pocket as he realized his glasses were on the kitchen counter. A nubby pencil was attached to the clipboard by a tangled string and Karen offered to read the information to him, but he insisted on taking care of it himself. She was uncomfortable being in a medical facility with him again, but they were there under better circumstances this time and she did her best to relax.

James started on the forms while Karen tried not to squirm in the uncomfortable waiting room chairs. Since he was a new patient, there were a lot of questions about his medical history. He began to read them aloud, "have you had any sexually transmitted diseases?" Karen laughed and prayed the elderly couple who sat a few seats away didn't hear him. He continued reading the array of medical conditions aloud and the two quietly laughed at his responses. Karen wiped tears from her eyes and begged him to stop.

It was a relief James that made light of his condition now that he was on the road to recovery. The longer they sat there waiting the more she stared at him in awe. "God is he handsome, and he's such a good man." She wondered how she got so lucky to find him in the first place. It was even sweeter that he was just as crazy about her. Thankfully, after another 10 minutes of waiting, he was called back for the scan.

While she sat alone in the waiting room, she remembered how close James was to death only a few weeks ago and she prayed he was never in danger like that again. He re-emerged after 30 minutes with a big smile, and they were free to go out for lunch. He took her hand as they walked out of the facility, and he had an extra pep in his step because the tech gave him a "looks good" with his thumbs up even though he wasn't supposed to say anything.

By the end of the week, James had completed the final round of medical appointments and received good news from his neurologist, Dr. Mancini. The flight didn't cause any further problems to his brain and he no longer needed weekly scans. Dr. Mancini requested a monthly visit for an additional three months, after which, he should be able to continue with his normal routines. The Doctor advised him against extreme activities such as off-road driving, sky diving, and diving off a high board to protect his fragile skull. Karen thought James made up that crazy list of dos and don'ts, but those were the actual instructions the doctor gave him. Since James didn't own a dirt bike, nor do they have a swimming pool at the beach house, she wasn't worried about him doing further damage to his head. No doubt, Karen would watch him like a hawk anyway to make sure he didn't overdo it because he was intent on getting back to work. Work, for James, meant overseas travel to check on his businesses as soon as he was able to arrange it. Karen didn't like the thought of him traveling alone to his offices in London, but she was not going to look that far ahead, and instead, focused on the day at hand.

Karen met her friend Jill at the Excelsor Polo club for lunch. The two shared a special bond, more like sisters than friends. The club looked exactly like Karen remembered it, pristine in every way. Floor-to-ceiling windows on the east side faced the polo grounds, and the windows on the west boasted a view of the fountain on the 18th hole from the second of four championship golf courses. Stretched across the far end of the room sat the heavy mahogany bar where executives sealed new deals over bourbons. Expensive liquor filled the floating brass shelves with the rarest brands proudly displayed on the highest shelf. Polished wine glasses lined the mirrored backdrop that made the room appear endless. Jill's meticulous attention to detail was everywhere, and she managed the sizeable property flawlessly. Thanks to those behind-the-scenes efforts, the Excelsor was a confidential haven for the wealthy clientele. Considering all the demands on her energies, Karen had no idea how Jill managed to keep her toned frame as fit as an Olympic athlete.

The polo grounds were picture perfect, and any horse would be lucky to trot across the soft sea of manicured grass. Keeping the Club in that pristine condition was no small feat due to the sheer size of the property that included polo grounds, stables, golf courses, clubhouse, restaurant, and a sizeable staff but Jill ran it like a well-oiled machine. She had the final say on all staff hires because of her unique ability to recognize talent in the most unlikely candidates, and everyone respected her opinion. It was her vision and expertise kept the Excelsor an exclusive destination.

It had been a while since the two friends had girl time and Karen really missed her company. Jill grew serious once they were seated. "Karen, thank you for getting Miguel back home safely. I tried not to worry about the three of you while you were away, but you were on my mind every minute of the day."

Jill's voice shook. Being so close, Karen felt the weight of her distress because Jill was usually so upbeat. "It had to be hard to wait for us, but we accomplished what we set out to do, and we're back safely. In fact, James and I are celebrating his clean bill of health tomorrow night on the beach. He wants to release Elizabeth's ashes into the ocean and he's planning a special dinner for the two of us."

"Sounds romantic, does he have an ulterior motive with the dinner, I mean, you've been dating long enough for an engagement?"

"Jill! It's too soon to think about a big commitment. We've only known each other for a year, and with his business travel and family tragedies, I still feel like we haven't dated much. Besides, you know I'm not the marrying kind!"

Jill had a sly smile, "just checking your temperature to see if you changed your mind about getting married. It would be okay if you softened on the idea."

"I don't need to be married but I did take a big step. I agreed to move in with him."

"Wow, that is a big step. Congratulations! Are you going to sell your condo?"

"No. I'm keeping it just in case things don't work out between us even though I can't imagine ever having a reason to leave him."

"Does James know you are keeping the condo?"

"He never asked about it and I hope he doesn't because I don't want him to think I'm not committed. I love that condo and worked hard to buy it in the first place. I don't want to dump it this soon and lose money on it."

"I'm really happy you agreed to move in with him. I have news too! I promised Miguel I would spend more overnights at his place. I started leaving a few items of clothing and toiletries behind and I'm excited about the possibility. Miguel knows I won't live with him without a commitment but I'm bending the rules just a little because I really hope to marry him some day. The time apart made me realize that he is the one."

Jill and Karen ordered splits of champagne to celebrate their relationships. Karen, who had been staring out the window, eyes unfocused, suddenly turned, "Jill, do you remember when I arrived in Florida? I had just lost my job with the Bureau, my life was a mess, and you told me change was right around the corner."

She nodded and they clanked champagne glasses toasting better times. "I will always be grateful for your friendship and, of course, the job at the Club", and their glasses clinked a second time.

The women caught up for another hour as they polished off another round of champagne. It was a delightful reunion. Karen promised to be back to work soon though Jill told her not to rush.

CHAPTER THREE

It had been at least three days since her former boss, Mark, left a message on Karen's cell phone and it was time to listen to it. Before her resignation from the Bureau, a call from her boss, would have prompted an immediate response, and she was oddly proud of herself for letting the message sit for a few days without listening to it. She pressed the button and heard the automated attendant announce three messages. Her heart beat a little faster when she heard Mark's voice coming through her phone. "Karen, it's Mark, I'm calling to see if you're available to consult on a case. It's about Devon Smith. I'd rather not go into the details over voice mail. My number hasn't changed, call me."

She dropped the phone on the couch, her heart beat faster with excitement. She hadn't thought about Heavy D since her father died when she was in High School. Devon Smith, a.k.a. "Heavy D", drove the car by her house the day her father was shot and killed on their front porch steps, but the police were never able to prove he was in the car. Heavy D had an airtight alibi, or he paid handsomely for the alibi, and the police failed to make any charges stick. The case went into the cold case files, but Karen always knew Heavy D was the one responsible for her father's death. Maybe the bureau will afford her the opportunity to get him after all. She knew Mark's number by heart and wondered whether she should call him now or after their dinner on the beach. If she waited, she would be distracted so she grabbed the phone and dialed Mark's personal number.

"Karen, it's been a long time since I heard your voice, how have you been?"

They carried on with a few pleasantries before she asked for details. "What do you have on Heavy D and what can I do for you?"

"That's what I was hoping you'd say. Devon Smith is moving drugs in and out of Newport; it's his new home base. He has a long-time companion named Gloria. I sent two agents in to get close to her but neither had any luck. Gloria is smart and doesn't easily trust anyone. She is also very loyal to Heavy D and it won't be easy to get close to her. I think you can do it better than anyone and once you get to know Gloria, you can feed us information. Specifically, where Heavy D goes and who he meets."

Karen was somewhat surprised "sounds like he grew up since the old days in the hood pushing pills and pot to kids. You know I'd be happy to help nail him, where are they now exactly?"

"I will send you photos and case history if your address is still the same."

"I have a new address, and someone is always there to accept a package."

"Karen, Heavy D lost upwards of 150 pounds and owns a chain of successful sporting goods stores. He's living in Newport in an expensive house near the waterfront and has a son named Markis. Markis attends boarding school and isn't around much but Heavy D is incredibly protective of him when he is home. The birth mother is deceased, and the girlfriend Gloria is a stepmom. Heavy D trusts her with his son's life and we think he trusts her with his business too. She's our only link at this point and we don't have much else to go on."

"I'll wait for the information to arrive before I make any promises. It was good talking to you again Mark."

"I'll expect you to fly to Boston for a briefing next week. The task force is run out of the Boston office. Call me Monday once you've read through the file."

She laid the phone on the coffee table and paced around the living room wondering what she just got herself into. How will James react when he hears she's consulting for the Bureau? They just agreed to a quiet life together. She paced while her mind searched for the right answer, but she already knew she couldn't live a quiet life without meaningful work. James couldn't stay at home either with the demands of his Company business so he couldn't expect her to stay home and be a housewife. She took a deep breath and walked out to the deck to call her long-term best friend, Brooke. No one understood Karen better than her childhood bestie and she needed to catch up with her anyway.

"Hey Karen, I've been dying to talk to you. The wedding is in three months, and I need to make sure you can still be my maid of honor."
"Of course I will, I promised you I would. How are the plans coming along?"
"Great, but the guest list is out of control. I want to keep it really small - more or less around 80 people - but every time we think of someone we forgot, it adds another 10 guests. I think we're somewhere around 150 people now and I'm freaking out!"
"Do you want a big wedding?
"You know I want a small one"
"If you want a small gathering, cut the list back to the original group. You shouldn't be introducing your new husband to anyone at the reception, and he shouldn't be introducing you to anyone for the first time either. It defeats the goal of an intimate gathering of close friends. If you or your soon to be husband John haven't met them, they're out!"
"That's why I love you Karen – that's exactly the advice I needed instead of telling me to relax like everyone else does! Are you bringing James to the wedding?"
"Definitely, and you'll love this - I actually agreed to move in with him"
"That's great news!" Brooke was truly overjoyed for her friend as she worried about Karen's happiness more than her own. It's just another endearing quality Karen appreciated about her oldest and dearest friend.
"Brooke, I have a dilemma. I got a call from the FBI, my old boss Mark asked me to consult on a case." Karen heard Brooke gasp. Brooke remembered the fateful case that caused Karen to resign from the bureau in the first place, Karen jumped back in quickly, "it has nothing to do with "that" case, it's someone completely different."
"Oh, okay, what do you want to do Karen?"
She answered quickly because she already knew what she was going to do. "Of course, I want to do it, but I'm worried about James' reaction." She usually made decisions in a vacuum but this time, it was different. This time, she had a partner to consider.
"If James loves you, he will support you." Brooke was right but Karen needed to hear someone else say it aloud for confirmation. She would find the right time to tell James, but it wasn't going to be during their special dinner.

Karen felt more at ease after talking to Brooke and had a greater sense of purpose after the call with Mark. She missed working with the FBI and while she appreciated the job Jill gave her as bar manager at the club, she longed for "real" work. The bartender/manager position kept her busy, but it certainly wasn't her professional calling. Once she helped Jill find someone suitable to replace her, she'd no longer have to feel guilty about missing shifts with no notice when she took time off unexpectedly. She sometimes joined James on a business trip and she'll need even more time away if she worked for the FBI. She hadn't liked leaving Jill in a bind when she left for Brazil because it was an open-ended absence. It was time to have a talk with her friend/current employer.

Karen put the FBI and club business on hold for the moment while she found something spectacular to wear for dinner. Kevin, James' driver, dropped her off at her condo where she scoured through her closets. She also wanted to pick up her car, check on her place after being away for so long and get back to James' house before dinner.

CHAPTER FOUR

James was pretty scarce all day. When Karen returned to the beach house after visiting the condo, Kevin was on his way out to pick up James. He was surprisingly reluctant to tell her where James was all day. The last time she spoke to James, he was doing a few errands and thought he would be home soon, so she knew he was up to something. Whatever he planned for their special night, Karen looked forward to the solitude on their beach front even though the tone of the evening was somber. They would share the sadness of Elizabeth's passing, and she would support James as he sent his daughter's ashes on a final journey home. It would be another major life event they would share with each other.

There was a white panel truck in the driveway and Karen tried to walk into the house without seeing what was being delivered. James had gone all out for their dinner, and she marveled at his thoughtfulness. Since the back of the house was all glass, it was hard to miss the intimate setup on the beach. A red tablecloth gently flapped in the light breeze. Fine china adorned the table for two set up on a raised platform to protect them from sinking into the sand. All of this effort was put forth just for the two of them. Three musicians tuned the strings on their instruments, and as Karen watched the workers quietly moving about on the beach, a warm breath brushed the back of her neck as James circled his arms around her waist. They stood close as his elaborate plan come together. He whispered, "I love you", produced a small box and said, "this matches your eyes."

Karen stared at the small black box and froze. He assured her it wasn't what she thought it was. She slowly opened the gift to find an enormous sapphire ring. It was perfect, a square four carat stone without any additional gems or ornate metal surrounding it. It was exactly her taste and she couldn't believe he picked out something that suited her so well. James had kept that sapphire for a long time. He planned to make a ring for Elizabeth when she graduated from college, but he thought it was even more fitting for Karen now. She was overwhelmed and winked as she promised him anything he wanted later that night.

Arm in arm, they descended the porch steps that led to their special table while James carried Elizabeth's ashes in his free arm. Karen snuck in a few quick peaks at her ring while the sun was still out and she was almost giddy. Their waiter brought two glasses of champagne, they slowly sipped, and placed the glasses on the table. James removed his shoes and Karen followed. He rolled up his pant legs and waded into the water just about knee-deep. The tide continued rolling tiny waves that licked the shore. James tipped the box on its side and the ashes slowly billowed out into the water. Karen kept a close distance behind him as he said goodbye to his daughter for the last time. The wind dusted the ashes evenly across the ocean surface and they encircled James as he remained stoic in the knee-deep water. He felt her tiny toddler arms wrapped around his knees, he heard her voice declaring herself an attorney as a teenager, and he saw that smile that warmed his heart when she graduated from law school summa cum laude. It was a movie he didn't want to end.

Ever so slowly, the ashes were pulled out into the sunset by the tide. Karen walked out further to join James. They weren't sure what prayer to recite because neither of them was particularly religious, but since they knew the Our Father, they said the prayer aloud as the tide methodically rippled away from them. James had a sense of peace now that Elizabeth's remains were near the home he shared with her for so many years. A tear ran down his masculine cheek and Karen held him as the sun slowly sank behind the horizon. They stood together while the final remains quietly floated out into deeper water until they faded from sight. When the hem of her dress fell into the water, she never moved a muscle.

They walked up to their table quietly and rinsed their feet. The waiter was attentive with towels and Karen put her shoes back on. She was content to remain barefoot but with the elaborate spread on the table, it was only proper to have on footwear during their elegant meal. They began with a small sampling of duck to which the champagne was a perfect accompaniment. Their next taste treat was ahi tuna on a bed of seaweed, spiced so sharply that her sinuses cleared instantly. She jumped a little when she tasted it and James beamed at her. He proudly watched her enjoy the next item on their menu and loved every minute of their special dinner. They weren't talking much as they savored every new taste sensation, small samples of duck, tuna, venison, oysters and their main entrée, a tiny lamb chop with a small dollop of truffle infused mashed potatoes. There was a lot of food but they weren't stuffed, just completely satisfied. All the while, the champagne flowed effortlessly.

James had one more surprise up his sleeve as the desert arrived. What a presentation! It was a flaming event on the dark beach as if they were on an exotic island vacation. They devoured every bite of the banana and rum concoction. The unique cross between the cold ice cream and the hot rum syrup created a taste explosion with every bite. After desert, Karen proposed a toast and thanked James for their dining event.

When dinner was over, she kicked her shoes off and proposed a walk on the beach like they did on their first date. He was happy to oblige and they walked and talked for another hour. It felt good to get in a little light exercise after the meal. She was anticipating the beach portion of the evening ending and getting back to the house where she will have James alone and naked. She kissed him on the shoreline and reminded him, his "treat" awaited once they got back to the house. He knew exactly what she meant and tossed her over his shoulder and ran towards the house. She gently beat on his back, "put me down, put me down, you know you're not supposed to be lifting anything heavy." With that he stopped as they laughed. Okay, she corrected, "I didn't mean I was heavy, I just meant you had a big meal, you're not 100%, and you shouldn't be running and carrying me." They continued kissing as they made their way up to the porch and into the house.

Once inside the house they made love as if they were the last two people on earth. They started in the living room and slowly made their way to the bedroom satisfying the insatiable hunger for each other that had been building throughout their dinner. They had a rare passion between them, one that hadn't diminished no matter how many times they made love. Completely spent, Karen lay in his arms while her breathing slowed. Her body melted into the mattress as she drifted off into restful sleep.

CHAPTER FIVE

Karen was first to wake. She snuck out of bed and went to the kitchen to get the coffee brewed. The high-pitched beep alerted her to the full pot, and she poured a steamy mug full. After wrapping a light blanket around her shoulders, she carefully balanced the full mug while she walked out to the deck, the steam rising from the cup in the chilly morning air. It was peaceful and quiet. She stared at her ring knowing she could never afford anything like it and wore it with pride. Her mind wandered until she was interrupted by a seagull squawking overhead. He made a racket overhead and interrupted her little sanctuary. Once he realized she had no food to share, he finally moved along down the beach. She watched the fishing boats headed out to sea for the day and faintly saw the pleasure boats being loaded into the water from the boat launch less than a mile away. She breathed in a few more salty breaths of the crisp morning air and returned inside for more coffee.

James was up cooking breakfast so she topped off his coffee before she poured her second cup. She dangled her ring under his nose while he cooked.

"Looks like someone must really love you to give you a ring like that." Using her best smartass voice, she replied, "I'm worth it."

He turned with a sly grin and said, "You certainly are."

As they sat at the table enjoying poached eggs and multi-grain English muffins, Karen decided to get the elephant off her chest. "I heard from Mark. He wants me to consult on a case."

James clenched his teeth slightly, "you don't need to work Karen, but I will support whatever you decide as long as you're not putting yourself in danger. You said, consult. What does a consultant do for the FBI, exactly? Will you work for them from home?"

"It's field work, but it's only one case. I'll have to temporarily reside in Newport."

"Newport, California or Newport, Rhode Island?"

"Rhode Island and I will have to spend a lot of time there. I need to get close to a woman to gather information. I haven't said yes yet, I wanted to talk to you about it first."

"If it was up to me, I'd rather you never leave the State of Florida ever again but it's not up to me. You mentioned a woman, is the woman the one they are after?"

"No, they are after her boyfriend, you know the type, drug trafficker with lots of money who thinks no one knows what he's really doing."

"That's what I was afraid of."

"James, I can't get into the details but this case is different. The drug trafficker is the bastard who killed my father. While I haven't said yes, there really is no way I can walk away from this one. I should get a package of information sometime today and I didn't want to bring it up during dinner last night but didn't want to delay telling you any longer."

In the end, James was supportive just as she hoped he would be. He volunteered to help her stake out Newport and she found the gesture endearing. After waiting for most of the day, the package finally arrived at 2:30 PM. As she pored over the photographs, she realized Mark was right, she wouldn't have recognized Devon Smith, if she passed him on the street. He was no longer the "Heavy D" punk she remembered. He looked like someone who could have a proper name like Devon Smith. His muscular body and shaved shiny head, befitted of a businessman, not a drug dealer. While he was always a big guy, she never knew he had a shape under all the excess weight he carried as a teen. She continued combing through the information and found a picture of his son Markis. He was a cute little boy. His girlfriend Gloria was a beautiful African American woman who ran an art boutique on the waterfront and looked suitably matched to the new Devon persona. They looked like a power couple and with Markis in tow, there appeared to be a successful family unit.

At first glance, Gloria didn't look like she grew up with an underprivileged childhood and Karen couldn't understand why a woman like that would attach herself to someone like Heavy D. The more she read, the more she wanted to get started. She would attend a briefing in Boston as long as it was not this coming Wednesday. James had an appointment with a specialist that day. Because his head was slammed against a concrete floor with such force, the doctor had to check his ears to ensure none of the small bones inside were dislodged. She called Mark that very afternoon because there was no reason to wait any longer. He promised to send plane tickets for a flight on Friday. Karen had to talk with Jill about finding a replacement at the Club, get things set at her condo, and make sure James attended his appointment, the last being the most important on her list.

Monday, after a run, Karen swung by the Club where Jill was busy as usual. Jill opened the conversation with an invitation for dinner on Wednesday with her and Miguel. Jill worked a half-day on Wednesdays and spent those afternoons teaching spin classes at the gym. Karen accepted without checking James' schedule because she already knew he was free. When Karen brought up the bar schedule, Jill told her not to rush back. The women laughed awkwardly and Karen said she was getting a complex because this was the second-time Jill told her not to rush back to work.

Jill quickly confessed. She had found a replacement bar manager while Karen was in Brazil, it was the first time someone worded out, and even better, Jill liked him. Karen was relieved knowing her resignation would not cause any problems as she proceeded to tell her friend about her new endeavor with the FBI.

"It's the right place for you now Karen, you can live here and go anywhere they need you but the best part is, you only go when you want to go. As a consultant, you have the best of both worlds. Let's meet at Miguel's Wednesday night. Do you know where he lives?"
"I don't know where he lives but I'm sure we'll find it without too much trouble. Send me the address and we'll see you around 7:30." Karen didn't think it was prudent for Jill to know she had already been inside Miguel's condo having broken in a few months ago looking for information while investigating Elizabeth's death. Karen suspected Miguel knew more than he let on at the time because of his family connection to the twins, but that secret break-in was locked away in her memory.

CHAPTER SIX

  Karen checked off another task on the "James clean bill of health" list after his morning doctor visit. Dinner was at Miguel's at 7:00 and it was more like a family reunion than just dinner. When they arrived at Miguel's, to no one's surprise, they were right at home comfortable and relaxed among the friends. After dinner, Miguel invited James to the balcony for a cigar and he relayed the most recent news from Brazil. Miguel didn't say much since they agreed not to speak of their trip again but he provided James an update to quell any worries he or Karen may have had.

  Once home from dinner, James relayed the conversation to Karen almost word for word. Jorge, the twins' father, returned to Brazil after a lengthy trip to Spain only to realize his sons hadn't been seen for over a week. He assumed the boys took the family yacht for a joy ride, but when they weren't reachable, he dispatched a small army to find them. Crews searched the surrounding harbor and spread out along the coastline looking for information. Miguel was confident no one saw them. There were no other boats in the area when they landed on the yacht prior to the explosion, and they left just as quickly before the boat exploded with the twins aboard. Even if a crew member miraculously survived, which was unlikely, no one on board saw Karen and Miguel land on the deck that day. The news didn't sit well with Karen but she pushed aside the impending dread that arose from the conversation.

  On Friday morning, Karen was up early raring to go. James supported her decision to return to work but wished it wasn't so soon after returning to Florida. He kept his thoughts to himself however and accompanied her to the airport for her 8:30 AM flight from Orlando to

Boston's Logan airport. After an uneventful flight, Karen found a young cadet waiting for her at the airport. Tess, who insisted on calling Karen "ma'am", was dressed in plain clothes but had the air of a rookie agent as she stood with an erect stance and spoke in quick short sentences. Tess drove them to the field office where Karen was given a visitor's badge. She did her best to remain friendly as the two women wove their way through the maze of hallways toward the briefing room. Tess followed Karen into the ladies' room and stood a bit too close as Karen washed her hands. Karen promised she wasn't going anywhere alone but needed a little elbowroom and Tess apologized for hovering. Tess reminded Karen somewhat of herself when she first arrived at the bureau eager and determined. A new agent tries so hard to impress the brass to garner a field assignment, and Karen promised to put in a word of support for Tess before she left the facility.

Mark leapt up from behind his desk when he saw Karen. They shook hands at first and then hugged each other, clearly happy to be working together again. They proceeded to the conference room where Mark introduced her as a "Special Investigator with long ties to the FBI." She didn't recognize anyone in the room but was not surprised by the new faces since it had been years since she last attended a briefing. It would only be a matter of time before the team learned about her prior stint at the Bureau. She almost blew a case the task force spent years building because she allowed a friend to get too involved in the case which was the ultimate cause of her resignation. Back then, she lost the trust of her team and had no choice but to resign from the job she loved despite Mark's insistence she stay. She hoped the new team would trust her now that she was back on board as a consultant, and she didn't plan to discuss her past with anyone unless it was absolutely necessary.

After spending three hours in the conference room with the taskforce Karen was up to speed on the case. Devon Smith was under suspicion for drug trafficking and for the disappearance of a college student. The longer she talked to the team and looked over the many photos pinned on the various boards in the room, the more motivated she was to help them arrest Devon Smith. The connections between the criminals were carefully detailed in front of her and she found Heavy D's life interesting in an odd sort of way. He was atop a sophisticated business with no formal education, his closest allies had been with him since childhood, and his net worth was nearing a billion. His movements had been tracked for two years; he never went anywhere alone, and his travel companions were always the same two men. Another disturbing part of the investigation included three college students who carried drugs for Heavy D's cartel and, while it wasn't confirmed yet, Karen was certain the evidence would prove their involvement. The students were "mules" used to transport drugs from South America to the U.S. Sadly, one of the students hadn't been seen since her last trip abroad. Karen met the group who investigated the missing student and their last known travel routes.

Gloria Simpson, Heavy D's girlfriend, wasn't under suspicion, per se, but she was very involved in Markis Smith's life. Heavy D's seven-year-old son attended the Ross Academy on Long Island. Markis' mother died when he was two and Heavy D raised him after her death. This school year was Markis' first year away at boarding school. He didn't want to go and caused trouble when he first got there but eventually settled in. Gloria was connected to Markis; therefore, Heavy D trusted her implicitly because he never left Markis alone with anyone else.

Mark gathered the team for a final announcement before they broke for the day, "I'm glad you've had a chance to meet Karen Anderson. Her role on the team is to gather intel on Devon Smith's movements by getting acquainted with Gloria. She will take up residence in the center of town and we will support her efforts. She will check in with me when she can. As you all remember, I sent two agents in to get close to Gloria and both were unsuccessful. I promise you, this time, we will bring Devon Smith down."
After Mark's pep talk, Tess magically appeared to escort Karen out of the facility. The two made small talk on the drive back to Logan.
"Ms. Anderson, do you miss being with the bureau?"
"Please call me Karen and yes, sometimes I miss being here. How long have you been an agent?"
"This is my second-year Ma'am."
"Keep up the good work Tess, listen and observe everything that goes on around you. You will get into the field one day soon and the more you pay attention, the more you will learn. And remember, sometimes people and events aren't always what they seem so you have to take your time, don't rush to judgment, and trust your gut. If something doesn't seem right, it probably isn't."

"Thank you Ma'am, I will remember that." They arrived at the Delta departures area and Tess raced to the side of the car to open the door before Karen reached for the handle. As Tess proudly stood in front of Karen by the open door, they shook hands and wished each other well. Tess looked like a college kid at first glance, but Karen noticed the resolve and deep sense of self behind her eyes.

CHAPTER SEVEN

Karen landed in Orlando and, Kevin, James' driver was there to meet her. She could have easily driven herself to the airport, but instead, followed James's advice, "Why drive when you don't have to." She missed James during their brief separation but he was there with open arms when she walked through the front door. After a long hug, she noticed the light meal set up on the patio. He knew her favorites after a long day, simple cheeses, meats, fruit, and crackers accompanied by a crisp cold glass of white wine. He offered a suggestion she wasn't expecting.

"I picked up a condo in Newport and we can work together there. I need to meet my Board in London in a few weeks anyway and you can settle in while I'm away. That way, if you need a husband to fit in better around town, I'm your man!"

"I don't think Mark would appreciate you being involved, but he can't dictate who I live with. It's a great idea! The bureau promised to set me up in a condo, but something tells me your choice will be a lot nicer than anything the government provides."

They enjoyed the food and the ever so slight breeze that brushed across the table. "Before we get too excited about our new life in Newport, don't forget Brooke's wedding is right around the corner. I'm going to spend a week with her to help with last minute wedding plans. Knowing her like I do and her need to please everyone, the wedding will spin out of control if I'm not there to help keep her grounded. I can't wait to tell her about the surprise visit."

Karen called Brooke the next morning and, just as she thought, Brooke was relieved to hear Karen was on her way to help with the final plans. Karen quickly packed and flew up to Hartford to help her best pal. They had a great time, and hardly saw much of Brooke's fiancé the entire week since most of their wedding errands involved lunches out, or "after chore" drinks at various establishments around town. He was such a good sport, knowing how close the girls were, he didn't mind their longer than average outings for errands. They finalized the floral arrangements and stopped at a wine bar. They found the perfect guest book, finished off the seating arrangements, and celebrated their progress with champagne. They put together the favors for tables at the reception, then capped off the day with frozen drinks on an outdoor patio. They managed to go out for lunch or dinner almost every day, mixing in plenty of fun with the wedding plans. Brooke beamed through all of it and Karen couldn't be happier for her dear friend knowing she landed an amazing man. He had the patience of a saint and loved her just as she was. During their final wedding mission before the rehearsal dinner, they reminisced about the past knowing it was their last night alone.

Brooke started the conversation. "Could you imagine my life if I married Bob, I shudder to think about it knowing where I am now."
"Let's not look back Brooke, your life worked out the way it was supposed to and I can't wait to see you walk down the aisle"
"Will you and James ever get married? I want to know my best friend is happy too."
"I am very happy Brooke, and I don't need to be married. James is the one for me and I wouldn't change a thing about our relationship."
"I was hoping you changed your mind since you're wearing that gigantic ring he gave you!"
"You never give up, do you?" It was endearing that Brooke wanted to see her best friend married now that she was getting married herself. Someday Brooke will accept that marriage wasn't a priority for Karen.

James arrived at the rehearsal dinner and looked so handsome Karen caught her breath. It was a delightful night out with the wedding party. The group dined at a private table for eight and gorged on seafood. Brooke had a few more drinks than usual and became increasingly emotional as the night progressed. John remained steadfast by her side as she thanked everyone for being part of her special night.

She made a tearful toast and Karen welled up as her friend expressed her gratitude. Karen passed on the final round of coffee with Amaretto after the meal knowing she wouldn't sleep a wink if she had caffeine that late at night.

While Karen thoroughly enjoyed dinner and the new friends she made, she wrestled with a request the wedding party received from the priest. Earlier that day at the church rehearsal, the priest asked all those participating in the wedding to attend confession before the ceremony. Being raised a Catholic, Karen was comfortable with confession in years past, but the opposite was true now; she was against telling a priest about her actions as an agent. She thought about it all day before she decided. Brook won't mind either way because she wasn't religious, but Karen had to tell her before they left for the night. As usual, Brooke understood, and no matter what the Priest said Karen, wasn't making a confession before the ceremony.

Karen arrived at Brooke's house the next morning two hours before the ceremony to help her get ready. Brook greeted her at the door in her underwear while the makeup artist pestered her to sit still for 10 minutes. Music blared from a speaker in the kitchen and Brooke offered Karen a glass of champagne. A padded silk hanger held the wedding dress off the floor in the bedroom closet doorway. The off-the-shoulder white gown was stunning. The crystal beading glistened across the fitted bodice while Toole flared on the lower half that included a small 12-inch train. When Brook finally slipped into the beautiful dress, Karen was speechless. She appreciated how lucky she was because her friend was as beautiful on the inside as she was on the outside. Brooke gave Karen a lovely pair of pearl earrings to wear with her maid of honor dress as well as a two-page handwritten note begging Karen to read it later to prevent tears from ruining their freshly applied makeup. Karen agreed and put the note into her handbag, a whiff of curiosity wafting through her head.

The ceremony was touching and the reception was a blast. The band played until 2:00 am and it didn't seem like anyone left the reception early. James and Karen danced the night away and Brooke gave her the eye of approval every time she spotted them together on the dance floor. Tipsy women lustfully eyed James as he moved around the reception hall, and Karen noticed every one of them. The longer they danced the more Karen wanted to get him back to their hotel room to strip off his clothes and make hot passionate love to him.

When the band finally concluded and everyone headed back to the hotel, Brooke asked Karen to swing by her room for a nightcap. Karen whispered to her, "I'm going to have my own party with James, and I will see you in the morning."
"Go get 'em girl – love you" she said, and they went their separate ways.

Karen was all over James as the elevator whisked them up to their suite. He reminded her of the cameras overhead but she didn't care. She wanted him so badly she could have had sex with him right there in the elevator. James fumbled with the key and before the door to their hotel room closed, her dress dropped to the floor. She leapt onto the bed and James slowly undressed while he watched her lay naked waiting.

The two lovers rolled around in bed together for hours and fell asleep exhausted in each other's arms. After all the champagne she drank at the wedding, Karen was relieved she woke without a hangover the next morning. James held her tightly and quietly whispered to go back to sleep for another hour. She wasn't tired and rolled on top of him intent on reigniting their last session. He was a happy and willing participant, as usual. Wrapped in his arms, she held his face in her hands and quietly mouthed the words, "I love you".

Before she got out of bed, she grabbed the sparkly handbag she used the night before, removed and unfolded Brooke's note, and settled on James' chest to read it aloud. Tears streamed down after the first sentence. Brooke and Karen went through a lot together growing up and Karen can't imagine a life without her trusted friend. The further she read, the more Brooke's note echoed the same sentiments Karen had for her. She couldn't begin to explain their unique bond but James knew it was special. "She's one in million James." He hugged her tightly and said, "So are you my dear." His voice quivered, and he cleared his throat. Without releasing the embrace, he quietly said, "I can't imagine my life without you" and tenderly kissed her forehead.

CHAPTER EIGHT

Once they said their good-byes at the hotel in Connecticut, they drove just over an hour until they crossed the Newport Bridge. It's actually the Claiborne Pell Bridge but the locals called it the Newport Bridge, and everyone knew what that meant. Newport wasn't like other New England towns. It had a "Kennedy" feel to it, meaning it's a sailor's paradise where very wealthy people came to relax. Since Newport was close to being an island, there were boats everywhere. As Karen watched the charming seascape go by through the passenger side window, she was somewhat surprised Heavy D would settle in an area like Newport. She had even more trouble imagining him fitting into an old money town like this.

In the Mercedes convertible, James turned right on to America's Cup Avenue and before long they arrived at the Vanderbilt Residences. James had the same grin she'd seen many times before so that meant whatever he picked out for their home away from home was likely spectacular. He worked miracles in short order. It wasn't that long ago he promised a comfortable place to live while she worked in Newport and, voila, they were about to get a new set of keys.

They followed the signs to the sales office after walking ¾ way around a beautiful porch, entered through the front door into a spacious lobby/library welcome area, and Karen knew right away she would be really comfortable living there. The sales office looked more like a living room in a fine home with a perfect blend of antiques and modern accents. Before they finished taking in all the sights, they were interrupted by a lovely young woman in a grey silk suit. Rebecca greeted them with a handshake, "Welcome James and Karen. We've been expecting you, let me show you to your new home." Rebecca handed the keys to James, never asked for identification and there was no paperwork to sign. They were escorted to their unit, and Rebecca pointed out the amenities on the way.

Their unit number was 111D and it not only faced the water, but half of the living space was actually built IN the water supported atop cement pylons. It was 1800 square feet but seemed bigger inside because of all the windows. The décor was thoughtfully selected and true to the classic style of the area. An oversized leather sectional was the only piece of big furniture in the center of the living room. It was a perfect place to get swallowed up while watching a movie under a blanket on a stormy night.

James squeezed Karen's shoulder and said, "I didn't fill up the walls with artwork, I thought you might want to pick up something up while I'm traveling."

It didn't escape Karen's thoughts that James gave her a chance to add a woman's touch to the place. It also gave her a reason to visit Gloria's shop without being so obvious. She pushed the work thoughts away and refocused on the remainder of the tour around their new digs.

The kitchen was modern and sleek. The stainless-steel appliances gleamed and the marble counters were black with white/sliver specs that picked up the overhead lights, and colors danced as they walked around the island. The refrigerator was stocked with food as was the all-important wine refrigerator. The off-white cabinets didn't need to be opened because she already knew they contained everything she needed. An oversized kitchen island had three stools and a huge bowl of lemons right in the center. It smelled so fresh and clean she didn't want to cook or even eat in the pristine kitchen.

They continued down a hall to find his/her separate offices which, in other units, those two rooms were designated as bedrooms. James' office had a massive floor to ceiling bookcase on the entire wall behind his desk. The desk was a simple antique table without drawers and his sleek dark brown leather chair completed the look. Two flat screen TVs were mounted on the opposite wall to keep track of different stock exchanges. It was a blend of antiques and modern technology that emitted a successful masculine vibe that was all James.

Karen's office was perfectly suited to her tastes. The biggest window was full of leafy green hanging plants. A light wood desk with double sided drawers was complimented by a dark green chair that adjusted to the contours of her body. Dimmable canned lights in the ceiling and small lamps throughout the room provided ambiance adjustable to fit her mood. In front of the desk lay a hand-woven rug that looked oddly familiar.

"Is that the rug I saw at the market when we were in Brazil?"

"It is! You said you liked it so I made a few calls."

"I love it.... and I love you!"

The master bedroom was on the top floor completely surrounded by glass. A circular window in the master bath allowed the bather to see the harbor from the tub. Karen climbed into the two-person soaker tub fully dressed and asked James,

"How do I get in and out of this tub without everyone in Newport seeing me?"

He laughed, "The glass is treated on the outside, so you can see out but no one can see in."

"Hmmm, why don't you take off your clothes and I'll run outside and see if I can see you?"

"You're going to have to trust me on this one."

She gave him a big hug, "I have no idea how you arranged something like this so quickly without ever asking for any input from me. I can't keep a secret to save my life when it's a surprise for you, and I had no idea you bought a place, but this it's amazing!"

James was flying out in the morning and they laid arm in arm on the huge bed going over his travel schedule. Though she was sad he was leaving so soon after they arrived, Karen was eager to get to work and didn't protest for long. She quickly freshened up and they headed out to familiarize themselves with the downtown markets. Since their condo faced the waterfront, it was an easy walk down a few steps, through a locked gate and on to the floating dock. They meandered by yachts moored along the dock picking out their favorites until they came upon a small footbridge. The access to the mainland took them no more than 10 minutes from their condo.

The waterfront had everything: restaurants, bakeries, a coffee house, specialty shops/boutiques and art galleries. Karen kept an eye out for Gloria's boutique "Worthy Endeavors" while they casually strolled around the cobble stoned streets. She was pretty hungry; it was after 5:00 pm and they hadn't eaten since they left the hotel that morning. They poked around for 30 more minutes, read the menus posted outside the restaurants, until they found the right Italian spot. Uncle Tony's, a double Michelin star eatery, was one of the oldest on the waterfront. It had a family casual atmosphere with exceptional food and service, and it was well-known that Emma Antusi, the 77-year-old owner, often cooked in her slippers! They dined on seafood at an outdoor table but it got a little chilly after the sun went down, so James asked the waiter to bring Karen a sweatshirt. There she sat wearing an XL Red Sweatshirt with an obnoxious logo. It had a white cartoon lobster holding a clam shell sporting a red and white checked bib atop the words Uncle Tony's Restorante. It was hardly a glamorous addition to her outfit, but it was warm, and she comfortably enjoyed the remainder of their fabulous bottle of wine. She had just enough to eat and wasn't too full to continue their walk around the waterfront after dinner.

Almost by accident, they found themselves in front of Worthy Endeavors. They went inside with the hopes of finding a piece of artwork for the condo. It was 7:45 pm and the shop closed at 8:00 pm. When they opened the heavy glass door, they heard, "good evening, how are you two tonight?" James answered, "We're fine thanks. We promise not to keep you late; we know we only have 15 minutes." "It's no problem, please take your time." They hadn't seen the woman who spoke and continued browsing around the store. James was drawn to two large oil paintings on the wall, one of which he thought would be perfect for his office. There were a few paintings Karen liked but they both returned their gaze back to the same piece. The painting was of a simple sailboat but there was something very special about it. The artist captured the calmness of the water and the sky indicated an afternoon/early evening time of day but the more you looked at one of the many small boats in the water, the more you want to be on that one boat and not the others. Karen found it fascinating that the artist could capture so much detail in that small boat even though it was set in such a large painting.

They were so absorbed in the oil painting, they didn't realize Gloria was standing behind them until she spoke, almost startling them.

"This work was done by a local artist, Jeremiah Wallingford. He grew up here and lives nearby. I am the only shop who carries his works."
"The only one?" James asked.

Gloria smiled, "Yes, Jeremiah is a little eccentric. He allows me to sell his works as long as I donate a portion of the sale to a charity of his choice. As you can see, he is very talented. He has the ability to capture your eye in the most unique way and you notice something different every time you look at it."

James nodded along with her in agreement and said, "We'd like to take this one home tonight."

"No problem, I can wrap it up for you. Are you here on vacation?"

"We just moved in to the Vanderbilt, my name is James and this is Karen."

"It's a pleasure to meet you, welcome to the neighborhood. I'm Gloria." After completing their $3200 purchase, they walked back to the condo with their first piece of art for their new summer home.

James was proud of himself after their interaction with Gloria. "Being an agent isn't that difficult, I already met Gloria for you!" "You're an agent at heart my dear that's for sure." She didn't allow James to get much sleep before he left. They couldn't hold each other close enough as they laid in bed looking at the stars through their bedroom window. "I wish you didn't have to go away tomorrow; I feel like we are on vacation." He kissed her forehead and said, "I will miss you more than you know."

CHAPTER NINE

Karen settled in to a comfortable routine while James was away. She stopped for a daily latte around 8:00 a.m. at quaint little bakery called - Patti-Cakes. The bakery was walking distance to Gloria's shop and the owner, Patti, and Karen became fast friends. Patti had been divorced for many years and opened the bakery to support her two children after her husband left them for another woman. "A younger woman" as Patti never forgot to remind anyone in earshot when she talked about her "asshole" ex-husband. Karen gave Patti a lot of credit because it wasn't easy to run a successful pastry shop in a high rent area like Newport. She was a gifted pastry chef however, and the aromas that emanated from the store brought people in all day long.

Patti and Karen chatted every morning over coffee. When they first met, Karen introduced herself as a private investigator chasing cheating husbands and Patti couldn't be more supportive of her career choice. Patti was the gossip queen of the district and gave Karen plenty of dirt on the business owners up and down the waterfront. Everyone knew Patti, whether they liked her or not. When Karen told Patti about the painting they just bought from Worthy Endeavors, she rambled on about Gloria. The women had been friends for years.

Gloria grew up in a working-class family, as did Patti, and Karen appreciated their similar backgrounds. All three women worked hard for what they had, understood the importance of an education, and were proud of their accomplishments, something else all three had in common though it was understood, but not discussed. Gloria had never married and had no children of her own. Every summer, Gloria spent a lot time with Heavy D's son Markis, and most people assumed he was her son. Gloria opened Worthy Endeavors with the last of her savings, and made it work. She lived on a boat and had no intention of getting a house on land even after the store was in the black. Gloria loved the water but Patti never understood why she stayed in those tight quarters and wasn't shy about proclaiming her disdain for the claustrophobia of the boat. Consequently, when Patti and Gloria got together, it was usually at the bakery.

Being the only single women business owners on the waterfront, Gloria and Patti got together at least once a week. Karen arrived at Patti-Cakes promptly at 8:00 am and Patti asked her to wait outside while she made their morning coffees. Patti approached the table with three plates of cinnamon strudels and Karen wondered if they were having company. To Karen's utter delight, Gloria joined them for coffee and pastry. Patti knew the two women would likely hit it off.

As Gloria approached the table, her stride was effortless, as though she didn't have a care in the world. Her clothes gently flowed in the breeze, and she carried herself with noticeable self-confidence. Patti gave her friend a hug and introduced Karen to Gloria. "Nice to see you again Gloria, we love the Wallingford." Patti was disappointed, "You said you bought a painting, but I didn't realize you already met each other, I was hoping to introduce the two of you."

Gloria calms her friend; "we don't know each other yet Patti. Karen and her husband bought a painting from my store last night." Karen was quick to correct her, "I'm not married, James is my... I'm not sure what to call a man I live with at my age. I guess he's my boyfriend." Patti chimed in, "you're a smart girl Karen, no need to get married if you're not planning a family." Gloria smiled and patted the top of her friends' hand, "we know Patti, men are swine" and the three laughed at Patti's expense.

The ladies continued their visit at a café table under a huge shade tree outside of Patti-Cakes until just after 9:00 a.m. when Gloria had to leave to open the store. "I have another Wallingford due any day Karen. Maybe we can discuss his newest work over a glass of wine?" Patti had to get back to work as well and Karen promised Gloria she would be in touch. Karen stayed at the table alone for a while longer and savored the remainder of the morning coffee. Her next call to Mark would put a smile on his face. She planned to wait another day or two before she followed up with Gloria for that glass of wine. There was no need to rush into their new-found friendship or raise unnecessary suspicion.

A dirty seagull squawked near Karen's table and she wondered what the fuss was about. She had no intention of sharing the remaining piece of her morning pastry with him, but the bird reminded her of Florida. She missed the beach house and even more, she missed her life there with James. As she watched the people mull about, she realized how easy it was to blend in here. Everyone looked they were from somewhere else. They traversed the cobblestone streets at a peaceful pace in their docksider shoes or sneakers, and it was incredibly relaxing to see so many people unhurried.

CHAPTER TEN

Just as she suspected, Mark was very impressed. He made the right decision to bring her on board and she heard the enthusiasm in his voice. "You're amazing Karen, in seemingly no time at all you're having drinks with Gloria. I wish you never left the bureau." They didn't talk long but it was an informative conversation. Mark filled her in on the latest news during the call. "Heavy D is having a 4th of July bash. Try to get an invite to see what you else you can learn. He has a sizeable property in Portsmouth and he spends a lot of time there. It's located about 30 minutes outside of downtown Newport where he has a stable full of horses and another residence. We have surveillance cameras hidden along the driveway and the people going in and out of that house are definitely not equestrians. We want to get someone inside that building when we know it's safe to poke around."

"I will work on an invite to the 4th of July party and see what I can do about getting access to the stables. I've ridden many times so I will figure something out."

Karen connected with James later that afternoon and as the conversation progressed, he grew notably worried over Karen's new relationship with Gloria. She promised him she was being careful, and casually ran through her day to assure him she was safe and currently fine without him.

"Enough talk about me, how are you feeling? Have you been resting, or have you been running non-stop since you got there?" James tried to be evasive, but she saw right through it. "The doctors said you had a clean bill of health but it wasn't long ago you were in the hospital and I don't want to hear from your assistant that you're in another hospital in a foreign country!

"Karen, please stop worrying, I'm not overdoing it, I promise."

"Okay, okay, I just miss you and I feel like I should be there watching out for you". Karen knew he was smiling.

"I'm glad you miss me, I will be home soon, and I love you. Now get out in our new town and protect everyone from the bad guys."

"I love you too - I'm on my way over to meet Gloria; I'm inviting her over for a drink tomorrow night."

"That's great and I promise I will only say this one more time - be careful."

Karen decided to invite Gloria in person rather than call her and she headed out to do just that. When she entered Worthy Endeavors, there were of patrons in the store but, though it was pretty crowded in the mid-afternoon, Gloria seemed happy to see her. Karen asked if she should come back, "oh no, no one looks really interested in buying anything, they're just browsing. How are you?"

"I'm good. I stopped by to invite you for a drink tomorrow night. I realize it's a Friday night and also short notice so I understand if you have plans. James is away all weekend and, while I can stay pretty busy during the week, the weekends get lonely without him."

"I'd love to come by – do you mind if it's late, say around 9:00? I'm staying open a little later now since the foot traffic is picking up with the warmer weather."

"No problem, I'll make a light snack."

"Don't go to a big fuss for me, wine is probably all I'll need after the week I've had."

Gloria asked Karen to hold on and walked to the back room to retrieve the new Wallingford. It was an amazing piece of art and once again, Karen was drawn into the painting. "Jeremiah's work is so captivating. I think I might have to take this one home as a surprise for James. He will be home late Sunday night and I will leave it wrapped in his office as a welcome home gift."

"Karen, you don't need to buy it tonight. Let me hang it first and you can look at it for a day or so and if you're still enchanted with it, buy it then."

"Why would you talk me out of a sale? You're not a very good businesswoman."

"I make sure all my customers are happy with their purchases and I wouldn't want my newest friend upset with something she bought at my store."

Karen was pleased Gloria called her a friend so soon and it was a perfect time to end the visit on a high note. "You are a wise woman Gloria; I will leave the painting with you for now and look at it a few more times before I buy it. I'm in 111D at the Vanderbilt, it's not hard to find since we are on the first floor. Our unit has the wrap around porch you can see from the marina, and a big silver wind chime hangs opposite the door. I'm looking forward to a little girl time. Should I include Patti?" Gloria quickly said, "She has teenagers and doesn't venture out on Friday nights to keep an eye on the girls so our get together can remain our little secret."

CHAPTER ELEVEN

It was a shame Gloria was part of the investigation because she seemed like a person Karen would befriend under different circumstances. She decided on a few easy homemade appetizers to serve with the wine that didn't require cooking since it was pretty warm in late June. Thankfully, it wasn't too humid allowing them to sit outside if they wanted. Gloria was due any minute and Karen had the CD player stocked with an array of music she aptly deemed "conversation music." The evening almost felt like a date because she was nervous and excited at the same time. She was energized to be working with the FBI again and being in Newport reminded her of home even though James wasn't in the next room.

Gloria closed the store at 9:00 and walked over to the condo by 9:10 pm. The new friends casually hugged and took up two stools at the kitchen island while Karen poured the wine. "I hope you like white?" "I do in the summer but wouldn't be caught dead drinking it in the winter." They laughed and continued drinking wine, snacking and talking just as friends do. They decided to remain at the kitchen island rather than carrying everything outside to the porch.

"Where is James?"
"He's in Europe, his corporate offices are in London and he travels a lot. I'm not thrilled about being apart so much and miss him every day he's away."
"I totally get it; my man is an absentee companion most of the time too though he rarely travels. He is just so busy that I don't see him as much

as I would like. Between his work and my hours at the store, we sometimes go days without seeing each other."

"What does he do? I'm sorry, I should at least ask you for his name before we start talking about him."

"His name is Devon. He owns the sporting good line, D. Sport. He's an entrepreneur and owns a lot of things that make money. He's incredibly private and would never talk about himself, but I'm proud to boast about his philanthropic work. He is a generous sponsor of the local boys and girls club, he built a new playground in our local park, and set up a scholarship fund for under privileged kids in our town. Behind all the expensive boats and old money, the struggling families are the ones who make the town work, and Devon never forgets about them. He grew up poor and, even though he never talks about it, I think he may have been homeless for a while. We have our differences, but I love him. It's hard to believe we've been together for three years already, and I have no idea where the time went."

Philanthropy isn't what Karen called his dedicated interests, but it made Gloria feel better and she didn't intend on probing any deeper into Heavy D's resume' during their initial solo visit. Gloria continued, "Do you have any children?"

"I don't, but James had a daughter Elizabeth who passed away last year. It's been a really difficult time for him as much as he tries to hide it."

"I'm so sorry to hear he lost his daughter, was she ill?"

"No, it's a story for another night. We finally laid her ashes to rest a few weeks ago. My poor guy also lost his son at a very young age. I don't know how a parent buries two children."

"Oh Karen! I'm so sorry for all the losses he's had to endure. I never had children of my own but Devon has a son. He's a dear sweet boy and he spends the summer with us. I can't wait to hug him. Sorry, that sounded insensitive after hearing about your loss."

"No need to apologize Gloria, Elizabeth and I didn't know each other very well, nor did we really ever become friends, and I never met James' son. That was long before the two of us met. Now I'm the one who sounding insensitive!"

"No need to explain, I hope you get to meet Little D. His name is Markis, he is a spitting image of his Dad, and loves being called Little Devon. We spend a lot of time together while Devon is working, and I try to make

Newport feel like home for him. He's had such a hard life for a little boy. After his mother died, he moved in with Devon and this year is his first year away at boarding school. It must be lonely for him being in a strange new place without any friends or family nearby. He is only 7 and I think he's too young to be sent away to school, but Devon wants the best for Markis and sometimes I bite my tongue to keep the peace. Markis idolizes his father and, since Devon is so busy most of the time, I try to be there for him to provide a sense of normalcy."

It was almost 11:00 pm and they both had enough wine.

"I don't know about you Karen, but I need to call it a night. I may be a little muddy tomorrow morning and I have to open the store at 8:00 am. I really should get going."

"I enjoyed having you over, it was fun, and we'll have to do it again."

"I agree, during the peak tourist season, I end up working a lot more than I want to and my nights out are few and few in between so this was a nice switch for me. Devon is having a 4th of July bash; you and James should come. It's his third annual party and it is a huge event."

"Thank you for the invite, we will be in town over the holiday and haven't made any plans yet."

Karen walked Gloria across the docks and they continued chatting about their men. She wished Gloria good luck with the patrons in the store the next day and thanked her again for the invite to the party. In turn, Gloria wished Karen a happy homecoming with James. Karen watched Gloria walk off into the darkness proud of her progress.

Karen hurriedly walked back to the house wondering if Heavy D will recognize her when Gloria introduces them for the first time at the party. It's been a little over 15 years since she last saw him, and she was doubtful she will look at all familiar to him after all these years. If it weren't for the FBI photos, she probably wouldn't have recognized him either and, after thinking about it, she wasn't all that concerned.

CHAPTER TWELVE

Karen couldn't believe she slept until 8:30 am the next morning and felt a bit like rip van winkle while the sunlight beamed brightly into the room. She usually arose between 5:30-6:00 AM; so, waking at 8:30 meant she really slept in. She lay in bed for a few more minutes picturing James' handsome face, missing his arms around her. She only had one more day alone before he was back home where he belonged. Life was off kilter when he traveled out of the country.

It was a beautiful summer day. Karen stopped by to see Patti for morning coffee, and per usual, Patti was worked up over an interaction with a customer, and everyone who passed by their table heard her rant and rave about it. Apparently, this "rude" customer drank more than half a cup of coffee then decided he didn't like it. He returned to the store, complained the cream soured because the coffee tasted awful, and he wanted his money back. Patti simply wasn't someone you challenged, and she never abided by the rule that "the customer was always right." In Patti Cakes, Patti was always right. She "helped" the customer by tasting the cream herself. She then poured hot coffee over the cream to show the customer that the cream didn't curdle so there was nothing wrong with it. He was, of course, embarrassed and offended by her theatrics. Patti told him he wasn't welcome back and finished her tirade as he excited the store. Her reaction was way over the top and the poor guy will buy coffee elsewhere next time. Karen found her cynicism funny in an odd sort of way. She also doubted Patti was really that rude but her animated stories were entertaining.

"Enough about the store, tell me how you became a private investigator. I think it's an exciting line of work, but can't imagine how you got into it?" Karen rarely talked about her past but felt comfortable enough with Patti to share a personal story about a harrowing relationship. Initially, Karen hoped to work for the FBI after her father's death, specifically to hold Heavy D accountable, but she couldn't tell Patti that half of the story. The other reason she opted for law enforcement was because she escaped an abusive relationship while she was in college. That relationship changed her life and left her even more resolved to get into the academy. Starting with the P.I. role, she adjusted the story thereafter for Patti's benefit.

Karen took a deep breath, and her facial expression changed as if she was about to relay something terribly painful. She looked at Patti seriously, "Patti, this is hard for me to talk about and I'm trusting you'll keep this between us." Patti's eyes widened and her head nodded rapidly up and down. Karen began the long sordid tale about the time she was involved with an older man, and thought she was deeply in love. She had been on her own for close to a year when she met him, and felt she was mature enough to recognize real love when she saw it. He was a lot older, almost 18 years her senior, and Karen thought it was exciting to be with someone who was that much older. She moved in with him after only two months of dating.

While Karen continued the difficult story, Patti remained enthralled. As the relationship progressed, her boyfriend was supportive of her career and encouraged her to set lofty goals. Once she obtained a Bachelor's degree, she planned to continue her education following with a Master's degree, then on to a PhD. His response was very telling, "I always wanted to be married to a Doctor and I hope you stay in school for as long as it takes." She found his support endearing and she hustled by working full-time while attending school at night. Her schedule kept her pretty isolated, and their wide circle of friends dwindled away until it was just the two of them. They spent all of their time alone, and family events were sparsely attended. Karen never stopped to realize that she was alienated and isolated from everyone she cared about.

They were three years into the relationship before she ever asked herself if she was truly happy. Being so busy, time flew by while she was absorbed in studies, school and work. Her boyfriend relished in knowing he had her all to himself and he also knew where she was every minute of the day. When she casually questioned their future together, a different person emerged. He was enraged she wanted to talk about their relationship, and, for the first time, he frightened her. She left his home and found a hotel nearby as a temporary respite. She couldn't afford much, and it wasn't a great hotel but it gave her time to think. Patti never moved a muscle while Karen bared her soul.

He begged Karen to come home. She reluctantly caved to the pressure and returned to his home. After a late-night argument, he bounded into the bedroom and pulled the covers tightly across her neck while he bellowed at her. She almost passed out from the lack of oxygen and somehow freed herself. Afterwards, he apologized and tried to make things right, but Karen knew their relationship was over for good. She left his house that night around midnight with her purse and car keys and spent the remainder of the night in a motel. They talked the next day and he said she could come by and pick up a few of her personal belongings. She's still not sure why she never told anyone she was going back to that house, but she went back to collect some clothes. She thought it would be okay since he seemed genuinely upset he frightened her, and most important, he promised to be out of the house while she was there.

When she arrived the next day, she had a pit in her stomach. Thankfully, his car was gone, and it appeared she had free access to the house to get her things, as promised. While packing, she heard the garage door open and froze. He came into the bedroom and wanted to talk while she packed. He picked up one of his golf clubs and practiced his swing right there in the bedroom disregarding her movements. She felt the whirr of the club go by her head and stopped in her tracks. She was careful to avoid getting hit until the next thing she remembered was crawling on the floor as she tried to get to her phone; her head and back seared with pain. Her once loving boyfriend clubbed her nearly to death in the bedroom that day. When questioned by the police, he claimed he didn't remember hitting her because he was so enraged, she was leaving. He said, "he lost it" and the rest of the events were a blur. Karen regained consciousness in the hospital where the nurse assured her he was arrested.

"I kept to myself for a long time after that since dating wasn't important anymore. I was safer alone." She felt stronger the more she talked about that awful time in her history. "I read a lot of books and talked to friends, but it was a long and difficult road to recovery. I moved and started over. I eventually finished school but never felt destined for a job in corporate America. After all I went through, I wanted to help other women who might be in a danger and that's why I became a private investigator." She also added that James was the first good relationship she had after that disaster which is probably why she deeply appreciated him and all of his goodness.

Patti was so caught up in the story she sobbed before Karen even finished. Patti told her at least three times she was proud of her, and that Karen was incredibly strong and self-reliant. Karen surprised herself by getting into that much detail about her past after only knowing Patti a few short weeks, but she knew Patti well enough to know Patti would relay every detail of what she just heard to Gloria next time they were together.

Karen confided in Patti for two reasons. First, it felt good to get that story out in the open and second, if Gloria described Karen to Heavy D as a battered woman who became an investigator he wouldn't think twice about her even if she looked remotely familiar at the party. Karen had to remove all suspicion in the unlikely event Heavy D recognized her. It was also a plus Karen won't have to retell the story to Gloria now that Patti knew. Patti clearly understood her reason for becoming a "private eye" after she heard that harrowing tale. If fact, the story wasn't a complete lie since Karen became an FBI agent in part because of that treacherous relationship.

CHAPTER THIRTEEN

Karen stopped by Worthy Endeavors to check on Gloria after their late night together. "Looks like you're busy today, hope the wine night didn't make it tough for you to get up this morning."
"I didn't have any trouble. It felt good to talk to another woman for a change and I woke up energized. Hopefully you felt the same. When is James coming back?"
"He returns tomorrow tonight, I can't wait to see him."
"I bet. Next time you're feeling lonely, we'll have drinks on my boat."

Karen left Worthy Endeavors after their brief encounter and strolled around the marina without a care in the world. She was somewhat surprised she befriended Gloria so easily. Her mind wandered as she walked and she smirked at her next thought, a surprise for James. Since he was flying into Boston, he had at least a ninety-minute drive back to Newport and there was no reason he should sit in the car all that time alone. She pictured the privacy screen slowly rising separating Kevin from the activities taking place in the back seat. Once the wall was up, she would show James just how much she missed him. A long ride alone together after not seeing each other for the past week was just what she needed. She picked up her pace and returned home.
Karen called Mark to share the good news; she secured an invite to the 4th of July party. She also planned a second one on one visit with Gloria later in the week. While Mark was happy with her progress, she was unsettled after the call. He passed along news about a missing college student, Rebecca Jones. The taskforce monitored local college student travel itineraries over spring break because Heavy D was known

to employ them as drug mules every year. The taskforce found three students who traveled to South America in a suspicious manner over the school break. They were singled out because they traveled alone to Columbia without any hotel reservations. They also took round about ways to get to and from the country in an effort to hide their tracks. The taskforce had yet to prove any of the three had ties to Heavy D's organization, but they were close. All three students were freshman, aged between 18-19 years old. They were carefully selected to carry drugs due to their financial vulnerability and need for quick cash to pay their mounting tuition bills. There were two males and one female from two different colleges who traveled alone to Cartagena Columbia during spring break this year.

Rebecca Jones attended Johnston & Wales University and barely scraped by financially; therefore, when she neglected to return to the University after spring break, her roommate wasn't alarmed by her absence. The roommate cooperated with the investigation, but she didn't know much about her friend's financial status or her travel plans. When Rebecca didn't return, the roommate assumed she withdrew from school and never thought to report her absence. The two young roommates came from different backgrounds and had different friends.

The members of the task force gathered a lot of information for the case file on Rebecca. They initially identified her through surveillance photos taken at the stables but when they tried to find her for questioning, they couldn't locate her. Never was she seen with Heavy D but she was seen at the stable with no apparent reason for being there. She never left the main house when she was on the property, and never rode a horse. Between the photographs at the stables and her travel patterns, she fit the profile of an organization drug mule. The other two students also photographed on the property toured the stable, and one actually rode a stallion around in a quick circle. They made it appear they were interested in riding, but it was an awkward encounter, and their intentions were obviously not above board.

During college spring break in March, all three passports were stamped going through customs in Mexico. It was tough to follow their digital footprints after that, and with obvious gaps in their travel routes, the FBI was unable to bring them in for questioning without more tangible evidence. Thus far, agents only surmised the travelers picked up another flight in Mexico and their passports were never stamped, or they had fake IDs. All three were found again through surveillance cameras as they walked through customs at the Cartagena airport but there wasn't a digital footprint of their flights or ground travel routes. Along with Homeland security and the TSA, the FBI was working with other foreign agencies, all sharing the goal of bringing down Heavy D's vast drug cartel.

CHAPTER FOURTEEN

As Karen traveled to Logan to meet James, she couldn't shake the thought of Rebecca Jones. How could a young woman be listed as missing for weeks without anyone looking for her? No calls to the police, no frantic family members sick with worry. Rebecca just disappeared without a trace but, after Karen learned more about her background, she wasn't that surprised. Rebecca was part of the foster care system and at 18 she was cast out on her own. Luckily, she was smart and landed in college on scholarship, but money was always her biggest challenge; therefore, Heavy D's promise of quick cash was too good of a deal to pass up. She probably never imagined herself as a drug runner with nowhere else to turn.

Karen was in James' sedan about to enter the Ted Williams tunnel as she neared the airport in Boston. Once the car grew darker in the tunnel, Karen was overcome by a wave of sadness for Rebecca. The sedan reemerged into the bright sunlight and her heart softened; James was going to be in the back seat of the car with her very soon. Kevin went inside the terminal to meet him, and Karen remained in the car. While Kevin tried to remain indifferent, he flashed her a small grin of approval. He appreciated the excitement she brought into James' otherwise very serious life. She told Kevin countless times, "every mogul needs a distraction." He shook his head and said nothing in rebuttal, but his smile was genuine. It was clear he appreciated Karen's sunny disposition.

James arrived at the passenger door and leaned in through window, "you are my favorite surprise. I called you but it went straight to voice mail and I hoped you might be her waiting for me."

"I have a bunch of surprises up my sleeve. I can hardly wait to get you home!" Kevin nodded to James, and they were quickly on the road back to the condo. The happy couple held hands and talked nonstop all the way home without missing a beat. Karen caught James up on the events in town and he absorbed every word. They longed to be laying in each other's arms soon.

Poor James. Before he even sat down and took off his shoes, Karen dragged him to his office for his first surprise. The new Wallingford leaned against the back of the couch wrapped in brown paper. Gloria delivered it before Karen left for the airport and she was happy to help with the surprise. James untied the twine around the brown paper and once the slight tension was relieved, the paper fell away and the painting was exposed. Just as she hoped, he loved it. He gave her a tight squeeze of thanks and then hugged her tightly a second time. He then picked her up off the floor and cradled her in his arms, "you take such good care of me and now I'm going to take care of you." They kissed passionately all the way to the bedroom as they shed clothing along the way.

CHAPTER FIFTEEN

Karen was the first new friend Gloria became acquainted with in a long time, and she looked forward to sharing it with Devon. His house was massive. Gloria spent most of her time between the family room and the kitchen while Devon tended to disappear into his office or as he called it, the "study." He was there behind closed doors when Gloria heard him talking on the phone. She crept in quietly through the double doors and he stopped talking when he saw her. He motioned her to leave and gestured with his hand - five minutes. She wondered what was so important that she can't be present while he was on the phone, but did as he asked, and quietly exited back through the double doors. Within a few minutes he yelled for her to return.

"How are you sweetheart?" Devon said with open arms.
Gloria hugged him and asked about the party preparations. "Are you using Jennie again this year?"
"I am, she's the only planner I trust. It's shaping up to be an even bigger bash this year than last year. The guest list grew pretty fast and, of course, Jennie asked for more money."
Gloria really looked forward to the gala and Devon spared no expense.
 "I met a woman in my shop a few weeks ago, and we have become fast friends. I invited her and her boyfriend to the party."
"You know you can invite anyone you want. Did she buy anything from you?"
"They bought a Wallingford painting. Then Karen came back to buy a second piece for her boyfriend James while he was away on business.

They own a condo in the Vanderbilt. They seemed nice and I met up with her after work for drinks."

"It sounds like they have money if they bought two paintings, knowing what you charge, and they also live at the Vanderbilt. That had to set them back a pretty penny."

"I guess so but Karen's not pretentious. I don't know her boyfriend that well."

Devon knew he was lucky to have Gloria in his life although he never told her so, and he was pleased she found a new friend.

"Hopefully Karen's not as nosey as your crazy friend Patti!"

"Devon, I assure you, she's not nosey. I went to her condo for drinks and half of their house is in the water. Maybe that's why we are friends because she likes the water as much as I do. "

"I wish you would just move in here and get off that God damn boat!"

Gloria smiled, "nice try, you know how much I love that boat. I spend most of my time here anyway. Is it really necessary that I give up my boat after working so hard to buy it in the first place?"

"I guess not but someday you're going to live here with me where you belong."

Devon's phone rang and, as nice as their conversation was, his mood changed, and he shooed Gloria out of the study for a second time. She walked out with the impressive list of invitees in hand. There were business owners, a senator, the mayor, an array of lawyers, and some of the upper crust of Newport. Oddly enough, other names on the guest list were the complete opposites: two bar owners, a liquor distributor and many of Devon's childhood friends from Connecticut. The charity chosen to benefit from this year's event was the Boys and Girls clubs of Newport. It's hard to think anyone in the area could be struggling but there were so many local kids with absentee parents because of their long work hours. The clubs gave them a place to go after school and Gloria was proud to co-host the party.

Devon received word that Rebecca Jones was missing. She never made it back to meet her handler at the airport, and that meant one of two things: either she didn't follow orders and was killed, or she was arrested in Columbia. In either case, there wasn't anything Heavy D could do about it, and the street value of the lost drugs wasn't enough for him to lose sleep over. He had two other mules with successful trips this year so Rebecca was nothing more than collateral damage. He was disappointed he lost money, but he never gave Rebecca another thought, she was just part of the cost of doing business.

CHAPTER SIXTEEN

Thousands of miles away on the Travares estate in Bahia Brazil, a worried father hired extra men to search for his missing sons who hadn't been seen for almost a month. Jorge Travares returned from a business trip in Spain to find his yacht and both sons gone. He hired a small army and enlisted the help of the local police. It was not unusual for his sons to take off without notice, but it wasn't customary for them to be gone for more than a few days without checking in with their father. The twins were grown men at 34, but neither held a job and their father provided the money and support they needed. They were as spoiled as two grown men could be.

After the first week, the police called off the search. They didn't have evidence to support foul play, therefore, they assumed the self-centered twins were on a whirlwind vacation. The Travares family was one of the richest in the state and the twins were well known by the local police, who nicknamed them, the "troublesome twosome." The duo was likely up to no good or simply slipped off somewhere to lavishly spend their fathers' money, and it wasn't worth their time.

Jorge was furious with the police's lame attempt to help and kept his security team focused on the boys. A yacht with a full crew doesn't fall off the face of the earth without a trace so, Jorge knew there was foul play. His security team had no leads, and no information. Jorge questioned them daily while his frustration deepened.

Meanwhile, a 65-foot fishing boat set out for its second trip of the season from a marina in Bahia. The small crew didn't have a successful haul the first time out and, after little rest, they hit the open seas once again. They spent the night on the boat and in the early morning hours, the captain was already underway toward their favorite finishing grounds almost 100 miles offshore. As the men prepared the deck, they noticed something floating in the water and the captain slowed the vessel for a closer look.

They were astonished to come upon a severely burned man clinging to what was left of a life raft as he floated helplessly in the vast Atlantic Ocean. He had been floating out there alone for just over 4 weeks and had run out of food and water two days before. He was barely alive. The crew devised a makeshift hoist the get injured man aboard. Two crewmembers jumped over the side rail and helped push the damaged man ever so carefully towards the boat. They tied ropes around a blanket for the hoist and carefully lifted man on deck. They tried to give him water, but the man didn't respond. There wasn't much else they could do to for someone so badly injured. The man hadn't spoken, and no one knew if he would even survive the long ride back to mainland, but they were determined to save him. The floating man laid on the deck half dead.

His face was so severely burned he looked like a sea monster. He couldn't see out of his left eye and his left ear was burned off. There was a ragged hole where his ear used to be with a small circle of charred cartilage around it. His shoulder had a huge gash starting near his neck and cascading down to his upper arm, and he had severe burns all down his left arm. He had two broken legs, a broken femur in one leg and a broken ankle and tibia in the other leg. He had three mangled fingers on his left hand that appeared to be no longer usable and everyone aboard the small boat wondered how he survived. They also wondered what could have possibly happened to him. He was in the middle of nowhere and his injuries were so severe, the crew stopped to pray assuming they would lose him any minute.

His face looked like a mask but surprisingly a faint whisper emerged through his scarred, parched lips. "I have money. HELP ME." The men on the boat were simple fishermen and looked at each other with raised eyebrows. They tried to make the half dead man comfortable atop a cot they made by with towels, nets, and a few haggard blankets. Floating Man eventually passed out and the crew was certain he would die before they made it back to shore. They were in a quandary, either save Floating man and hope for a reward, or toss him overboard since he was half dead anyway. They wanted to continue their trip, but they were honest, religious, men and couldn't send a man to his death without trying to help him. They changed course and returned to the mainland even though they spent all of their remaining funds on gas to help a stranger.

As the boat chugged back towards land, Floating Man faded in and out of consciousness. They offered him more water and slowly the injured man was able to ingest some fluids. With his one good hand, he grabbed on to one of the workers' arms and with a scratchy voice whispered, "you will be glad you helped me." No one really knew what to make of their discovery as they pushed their aging boat as fast as she could go to return to safety.

Floating Man stared at the powder blue sky from his cot. He knew he was going to make it. Smoke billowed from the boat's motor, but they pressed on. Floating Man closed his eyes and his thoughts raced to the dark corners of his mind. Revenge coursed through his veins, and he made himself a promise; he was going to find the people responsible and make them suffer just as he has suffered. He produced a wry half grin from the one side of his cheek capable of movement as the perpetrators burned while screaming for help. He dreamt of hideous ways to torture his captives and didn't speak to anyone on the boat for the remainder of the trip back to shore while his rage deepened.

The captain was starting to radio for help as the small fishing boat neared the dock at the Marina, but the floating man mumbled "no." He asked one of the men to come closer to and whispered a phone number, "call this number. Tell him you found me, and I need help." Josias, the Captain, cancelled the distress call, and asked the man, "Who are you sir? Who do I say we found?" Floating Man did his best to stay coherent but didn't have the strength to utter another word. Josias did as the man asked and called the designated phone number. When the line connected, he relayed the story quickly. "We found a man floating at sea, he gave me your number because he needs help. He is injured." Josias relayed their location and the voice on the other end simply said, "I'm on my way, don't move him, and don't call anyone."

Fifteen minutes after the phone call, a black van approached the docks, a doctor and nurse emerged from the van and hurriedly approached the boat. Everyone cleared the way for the medical team to care for Floating Man. It was odd that neither medical professional looked surprised to see the man in this horrifying state on the makeshift bedding. The nurse started an IV, applied dressings to his wounds and attached monitors while the doctor administered as much medical care as he could there on the deck of the small boat.

Behind them loomed a giant who stood at least 6'6" and was as broad as he was tall. He towered over Josias who was barely 5'8" with a slight build. The man asked for the captain. "I'm here sir." The giant man slowly removed a thick envelope of cash from the breast pocket of his expensive blazer. He handed the money to Josias. "Split this with your crew, we are indebted to you for finding him and bringing him back to shore." Josias stumbled to ask, "Who is this man?" The giant didn't answer.

Floating Man was placed on to a gurney and carefully lifted into the awaiting van. The heavy doors closed and the team drove away from the dock without raising suspicion in the harbor. Once out of the inner harbor, the driver made a quick exit to the highway and the van quickly sped off with its precious cargo.

Josias was instructed to take his crew into town for a proper meal and he wasn't to mention any of the events that took place on board to anyone. The giant was clear – keep the meeting a secret and if anyone talked, they will suffer. The man stayed behind after the van left to make sure the small boat was refilled with gas while the crew ate so they could resume their trip when they returned to the boat. The man tipped his head slightly to Josias as the crew prepared to leave for town, "we are grateful you returned our friend."

The giant man paid a deck hand who ensured the small fishing vessel was readied for another trip. The coolers on board were stocked with food, a leaky hose was replaced, and the gas tanks were filled under the watchful eyes of the giant. During dinner, the fishing crew agreed to keep their mouths shut after they split the handsome payment. It was obvious the man they rescued had very powerful friends. The new-found money afforded them more than they could have earned from their catch, and they looked forward to sharing their good fortune with their families upon return. Whether they caught any fish or not, each member pocketed $5,000; a small fortune to men who just barely eked out a meager living from the sea.

CHAPTER SEVENTEEN

Floating man was eventually transported by helicopter to the trauma unit at the Hospital do Surburbio in downtown Salvador. He never regained consciousness after he left the dock. The helicopter landed on the roof of the hospital and the trauma team rushed him inside for treatment. They assessed his condition quickly and opted to repair his internal injuries first, then address his broken extremities. His legs needed to be immobilized after the bones were reset though they couldn't save the mangled fingers on his left hand. It was a miracle he made it through the long, complicated surgery and, though the doctors hoped he would eventually recover, only time would tell. The man remained in a coma in the ICU.

The menacing giant, Ricardo, who met Captain Josias at the dock, made the arrangements for the burned man's safe travel. Ricardo was the head of Jorge Travares' security team. Jorge was Miguel's uncle, and neither he nor Ricardo ever suspected his nephew was responsible for the disappearance of his own cousins. Ricardo had been the head of security for Jorge's family for 17 years and Jorge trusted him implicitly, but Ricardo knew Jorge Travares was a man you didn't disappoint and he spare no expense in the search. Unbeknownst to Ricardo, he had actually hired the burned man as a cook on the yacht but hadn't recognized him in his current condition, so his identity was still a mystery to everyone. Ricardo hoped he was one of the twins, but he didn't alert his boss until he had confirmation.

The medical team provided around the clock care for their "Fulano," or John Doe, as the burned man was aptly named. Ricardo was the only contact on his behalf. He said the unknown man was a friend, but since the Fulano remained unconscious, Ricardo couldn't confirm his identity until the bandages were removed to see his face. He assured payment for the patients' treatment but, until then, there wasn't much more to do but wait. The surgeries were risky and the Fulano had a long and complicated treatment plan ahead.

When the surgeons emerged with another update, Ricardo remained stoic while he heard somewhat positive news. They made no promises and Ricardo nodded emotionlessly while the doctors updated him on Fulano's condition. Once the doctors exited through the automatic doors, Ricardo decided to bring Jorge into the loop. Jorge needed to know that the man in the ICU could be his son but Ricardo couldn't confirm if it was or wasn't one of the boys. Jorge left for the hospital in a flash even though Ricardo insisted he wait at home for more news. Jorge believed he would instinctively know if the person in the bed was his flesh and blood no matter how unrecognizable he was.

Jorge arrived at the hospital and Ricardo accompanied him into the ICU. The room was quiet except for the rhythmic beep of monitors around every bed. When Jorge approached the man's bedside, he was shocked by what he saw. He wasn't prepared for the dire condition the Fulano was in. Most of his face was wrapped in bandages so Jorge could only see one closed eye. His legs had metal contraptions poking through his skin with rods and screws holding them together and his hand was fully wrapped in a bandage. He was on a respirator and Jorge didn't want to touch him. Much to his chagrin, he didn't know if the ICU patient was one of the twins even though he hoped it to be true. Jorge wasn't quite sure what to do and Ricardo promised to remain at the hospital until the man came out of the coma.

Jorge agreed and left the hospital defeated. On the drive home, he prayed for a miracle for the unknown man in that hospital bed. He also prayed to be reunited with both of his sons though, in his heard, he knew this to be unlikely. If the man in the hospital bed was his son, he would spare no expense to get him back on his feet. He knew the police only paid him lip service when they told him the investigation into his sons' disappearance remained an open case. Jorge knew they stopped looking for them a long time ago, and for the first time, he had a sliver of hope.

The twins were always in trouble growing up, they were wild, spoiled and Jorge bought their way out of trouble every time. Jorge

Travares was a wealthy man in a poor country and that gave him an edge with a crooked police force. Jorge bought whatever he needed but all his money didn't help him find the twins. He was frustrated and angry for the remainder of the ride back to his estate.

CHAPTER EIGHTEEN

After being in a coma for 12 days, Fulano finally awoke. He was in and out of consciousness but the nurse assured Ricardo the patient should be off the ventilator soon and, once the tubes were removed from his mouth, they hoped he could speak. Ricardo approached the burned man's beside and introduced himself. Fulano looked at Ricardo with a blank, uncomprehending expression, he either didn't understand or couldn't hear and Ricardo quickly lost patience. The nurse sensed his frustration and suggested he return when the breathing tube was removed.

After an hour, Ricardo returned and waited next to the bed along with the nurse. She asked Fulano if he had a name. He swallowed wincing because any facial movement was excruciatingly painful. He mimed writing with a pen and the nurse retrieved a pad of paper and pen. The burned man trembled as he wrote without moving his head to look at the pad, and the only image he was able to scribble was a single letter. It took Ricardo and the nurse a minute to determine it was the letter "J" whereupon Ricardo asked him if the "J" means Jorge. Fulano blinked his one open eye and Ricardo immediately left the ICU to call Jorge.

Jorge returned to the hospital for a second time, and cautiously approached Fulano's beside. He was full of anticipation and hopeful it was his son but he wasn't convinced this stranger was a Travares. The man tried to talk but he could only whisper very slowly. Jorge remained patient and asked him, "Are you my son?" The burned man used all of his strength to say, "no." Jorge stared at the stranger and wished the word "no" wasn't in the room because there was no reason for him to stay there any longer. Jorge asked him who he was and why he wrote the letter J. The burned man muttered "Samuel" and Jorge replied, "I hope you get better Sir." Samuel tapped the pen on the paper before Jorge left his bedside. Jorge bent down closer as Samuel gave it all he had to whisper, "I know what happened." Jorge was stunned, "you know what happened to my sons?" "Yes." Samuel expended all the energy he had left for that short exchange and drifted back to sleep.

It was another two days before Samuel was moved to a single room in the burn unit. He no longer needed the constant monitoring in the ICU and was able to talk a little better. Jorge returned and Samuel saved his strength for the visit. He began slowly once Jorge was seated next to the bed. "I was on the yacht the day your sons died, Ricardo hired me as the cook. John Renaldo and Jon Giovanni were on the top deck of the boat. A group of men in a speedboat appeared out of nowhere and overtook the crew on your yacht." Samuel tried to prop himself up but didn't have the strength. The nurse gave him a sip of water and he continued. "Three of us were directed at gunpoint into a small life raft and set adrift. Within minutes, a helicopter landed on the upper deck, and a man and woman emerged. By then, Jon Gio and John Renaldo were in handcuffs. The men who took over the vessel returned to the speedboat and drove off pulling our raft about 100 yards away from the vessel. They dropped the tow line and sped off out of sight. The raft held me, the captain and a deck hand. We were far away but I could see the four people still on the deck. The captain had binoculars tied around his neck and I grabbed them to see your sons with the man and woman on the upper deck. They were the only ones left on the yacht."

Samuel needed another water break but continued the saga in a raspy tone. "The four had a drink of something and one of the boys spat at the man before the couple walked back to the helicopter. Once the helicopter was about a half mile away, there was a terrific explosion, and the yacht was gone. I have no idea how I survived; the other two in the raft with me were blown into the water from the impact and they never resurfaced. It is by the grace of God, and rations I found on the raft, that I am here to tell you what happened that day." Samuel was emotional "I can't thank you enough for all you have done for me in this hospital and I will be forever in your debt."

Jorge sat erect as Samuel retold the events of that horrifying day. When Samuel finished, Jorge tipped his hat and said, "The hospital will send the bills to me. Thank you for telling me about the explosion. I hope you are well very soon." His face deep in thought, Jorge slowly left the hospital with Ricardo a few steps behind him.

Jorge demanded Ricardo find out who were the couple on the boat that day. He was anguished and enraged and vowed to kill them himself. Once home, he worked tirelessly to uncover who met the twins on the yacht. His mind replayed Samuel's words about the "couple" on the boat. What kind of woman could this be? She must be an American because no Brazilian woman would be involved in something like that – it was man's work. Jorge remembered the Americans who traveled with Miguel. He thought the woman was outspoken and far too forward when he met her. He disliked her right from the start but tolerated her since she was a friend of Miguel's. It was a long shot but Jorge passed the information along to Ricardo for further investigation.

Ricardo returned to the hospital to check on Samuel. He brought along a picture of Miguel to see if Samuel recognized him as the man on deck the day the boat exploded. Even though Samuel was a distance away from the yacht, he was fairly certain the picture was of the man on the deck that day. He stared at the couple in disbelief because they were so brazen to harm a Travares family member. He was determined to remember what they looked like in case he had the chance to relay the information to Jorge one day.

When Jorge learned Miguel killed his own cousins, he was even more enraged and declared his nephew a dead man. Ricardo picked up one of Miguel's long-term trusted employees, Jamal Rendes. Ricard sought confirmation Miguel was on the yacht and he wanted the name of the woman with him. Jorge paced in his study as he awaited Ricardo's feedback. He poured a small glass of Tequila and, as he slowly sipped the alcohol, his blood ran cold with hatred.

Jamal Rendes worked for the other Travares family, Jorge's brother, Felix. Miguel's father employed Jamal for 10 years and Ricardo picked him up without any trouble. Ricardo made people talk, it was his specialty. After a few hours of torture Jamal would give up Miguel's family secrets, Ricardo was certain of it. Jamal was abducted quietly as he walked to his car in supermarket parking lot and was taken to a small storage facility on Jorge's estate. He hands were tied to a ceiling hook over his head and his feet tied to hooks bolted on to the floor so could stand but he couldn't move from that spot. Ricardo beat him about the body and head with a sock full of ball bearings. Ricardo swung the sock with ease at the beginning but as Jamal kept Miguel's whereabouts a secret, each additional blow was more forceful than the last. Jamal wasn't talking and Ricardo grew even more excited as the torture escalated.

Jamal had no idea what was to come next. Ricardo walked slowly over to a locked cabinet. He whistled while he unlocked the rusted metal door and retrieved a leather case of tools. He unzipped the case and removed a set of wire-cutters. He circled Jamal and asked the same question over and over taunting him as he tapped the tool on his shoulder. He said, "Jamal you can end this by telling me if Miguel was on the yacht the day his cousins died, you know the right answer, just tell me what I need to know and I will let you go."

Jamal wasn't stupid, "You aren't going to let me go and I have no idea what you are talking about, Miguel had friends visit and they were on vacation, I know nothing about a yacht or an explosion."

With no warning, Ricardo lopped off the top of Jamal's left index finger. Jamal screamed in agony and Ricardo reminded him, "you have 9 fingers left Jamal, you decide if you want them or not." Jamal remained silent as Ricardo lopped off the top of the pinky finger on Jamal's right hand.

Ricardo calmly continued as Jamal's blood dripped on his shoes, "Jamal, your young son is only 8. I can have him here in 20 minutes. Maybe you'll have more to say when you watch me beat him in front of you." With the threat on his son's life, Jamal caved and confirmed that it was Miguel Travares on the yacht that day. Miguel ordered the security team to overtake the yacht. They had orders to kill anyone who tried to stop them except for the twins. The Travares twins were to be kept subdued while the bomb was set in place. Once the yacht was secure, employees were taken off the yacht, and the bomb was secured in place, Miguel landed on the boat. The twins had killed his friend's daughter and he and Karen were on the boat to exact revenge. Ricardo made note of the name, "Karen" and Jamal continued. Miguel had a device in his pocket that activated the bomb remotely. Jamal pleaded for his life after he disclosed the truth about Miguel, but Ricardo had what he needed and ruthlessly shot him in the head. He wiped the gun clean, cut the ropes, and Jamal fell limp on to the dirty floor. Ricardo stepped over him and never looked back.

CHAPTER NINETEEN

It didn't take long for Jorge to learn the identity of the woman on the boat. Jorge remembered meeting Karen Anderson and James Caulfield, when they visited Miguel in Bahia earlier that year. Miguel's estate was next to Jorge's property and they met over dinner. Through a contact in Florida, Jorge learned Miguel had a steady girlfriend, Jill Freeman. Jorge ordered a hit on all four of them and had just the person in mind to get the job done. It frustrated him that Miguel never came to him about the twins. If they were involved in the death of his friends' daughter, they could have kept the matter in the family and resolved it between them. Now that it was confirmed that Miguel killed his cousins, the family bond was broken, and it was Jorge's responsibility to avenge his family.

Jorge telephoned a small garage in their local town where he asked for Axel Vascone. Axel went to school with the twins and spent eight years in the military. When he returned to civilian life, he helped his father manage the family business, a 2-bay service station. They repaired cars and sold gas. Axel was a skilled mechanic much like his father, but Axel had a side job that paid handsomely. He was a well-trained military sniper and marksman for hire. On top of that, he an antisocial personality disorder; therefore, leaving him with no remorse for the victims he killed, a perfect blend for a hired assassin. Jorge had utilized Axel's services before and he was worth the steep price of around $50,000 more or less depending on the risk level of the job.

Jorge was driven to the Vascone family station at 10:00 am the next morning. When he pulled up, Axel was attentively next to the car ready to open the door for him. Axel was a tall man with an average build, very lean, and not overly muscular. He shook hands with Jorge and they proceeded through the dirty service station into the cluttered office for a private conversation. The paper invoices scattered all over the desk and every available surface in the office had a light layer of grease so it was best left untouched. The tattered rug was in even worse condition. Axel wiped off the seat of the cracked leather guest chair and gestured for Jorge to sit, but he decided wisely to stand.

Axel's father continued to work on a car in the service bay when Jorge arrived. He watched the two men as they walked into the office, and no one spoke until the office door was closed. Mr. Vascone senior never questioned his son about the meeting that day, and he never asked where Axel got the extra money to help him out of debt the countless times he needed help. His son's military pension wasn't the source of the extra income, but he never wanted to know the truth. He owed thousands of dollars to a local loan shark after gambling money he never had but repaid the debt with Axel's help. He trusted his son, turned a blind eye to the meeting, and replaced a damaged hose on a customer's sedan.

Axel and Jorge spoke quietly in the office for only a few short minutes. Jorge relayed what he knew about the targets. "Jon Gio and John Rinaldo were killed by their cousin Miguel, and I want him and his friends taken care of. The information you need is in the envelope, and I have a plane ticket ready for you." Jorge placed a thick envelope atop a stack of dirty papers on the desk and Axel nodded as he assured Jorge, "it's done." Axel escorted Jorge back out to his car and watched as the sedan drove away into the busy street traffic then returned to the office, placed the envelope into his duffle bag, picked up a wrench, and returned to the car he was working on. Both men spent the remainder of the day completing repairs and never spoke of Jorge's visit.

CHAPTER TWENTY

After work, Axel retrieved the envelope from his duffle bag and spread the contents out on his small kitchen table. He refolded a matchbook under one of the legs to level the tabletop and gazed at the four photographs in the packet. Miguel Travares, Jorge's nephew, Karen Anderson, and James Caulfield III who lived together, and Jill Freeman, a companion of Miguel. All four lived in Boca Raton Florida. Jorge's instructions were very specific, and the kill order had to be followed. First was Jill, then James, Karen, and finally Miguel. Jorge wanted Miguel last as he watched his friends die one by one because of his actions. Axel never questioned who he killed or why anyone was targeted. His mission was to follow the wishes of his client, complete the job on time, and collect his fee. There was a special message for Miguel that was to be read aloud before he died, and Axel quickly memorized the hand-written note from Jorge. Axel had minimal travel experience outside of the military, and never set foot in the United States. He checked his passport's expiration date, researched the Boca Raton Florida area, and put his plan together.

Axel unlocked a floor safe in his bedroom closet and placed $5,000 in cash inside the safe. He made a stop at the bank on the way to work the next day and deposited an additional $5,000 into the stations' business account. Axel arrived at work at 8:00 am every day and his father arrived shortly thereafter. The men greeted each other with a nod and got to work. That morning however, Mr. Vascone Sr. was taken back because his son wanted to talk. Axel never called out to his father by name, nor did he use the words "Dad or Father", he simply stood near his father and waited until he had his attention, then he spoke. Mr.

Vascone knew his son's idiosyncrasies better than anyone, and Axel began, "I'm going away for a few days, but I will work on the white truck before I leave." Mr. Vascone Sr. didn't him where he was going because Axel didn't include it in the conversation. They were close as father and son, but Axel never spoke unless it was necessary, nor did he engage in lengthy discussions. Mr. Vascone Sr. loved his son none-the-less and appreciated him for qualities other than his conversational skills.

CHAPTER TWENTY-ONE

Axel's plane landed in Orlando uneventfully, and he approached the car rental desk for the keys to his weekly rental. As he waited for the paperwork, he saw children wearing Disney ears while they scurried through the airport, and he never understood the fascination with cartoons. He despised crowds and the tired cranky children dampened his mood. Once he signed the paperwork and had keys in hand, he hurried to the shuttle to escape the chaos in the airport. He longed for the solitude inside the car.

The GPS offered in the car was useless because the pre-programmed woman's voice who spewed directions grated on his nerves. Besides, it was safer to use maps and handwritten directions to avoid a digital footprint of his travels. He checked into the Sea Breeze Hotel in Boca Raton and picked up food from a local grocery store. He didn't eat at restaurants unless there was no other option. He preferred to eat alone and ensured his rented room had a microwave and small refrigerator so he could be self-contained during the trip. He watched TV for a short time and fell asleep with the glow from the TV screen the only light on in the room. His first stop the next day was The Excelsor Club, to locate Jill Freeman.

*****

The Excelsor Club opened early to accommodate morning golfers, horseback riders, polo players, and for those patrons who wanted to conduct business over breakfast. It was an exclusive club and the members enjoyed breakfast from 6:00 am – 11:00 AM before the main restaurant opened to the public at 11:00 AM every day.

The restaurant was located in the same building as the corporate offices and Jill Freeman's office was down the hall from there. She frequented the restaurant and bar throughout the day and kept in touch with staffers. Against his preference, Axel went to the Excelsor for lunch and ate at the bar. He arrived around noon to find it crowded but he was able to find a seat towards the end of the bar next to the waitress service station. He disliked mingling with the public, but he did what he had to do with a condescending "goes with the job" acceptance.

He ordered a salmon salad and lemonade while he kept an eye out for Jill. Having studied her picture so closely, he was confident he would recognize her instantly if she entered the bar. He paid his tab and while waiting for change, he saw her. She acknowledged many of the patrons and walked behind the bar to speak with the bar manager about an upcoming event. She was all business and Axel appreciated how serious she was. Jill never concealed her conversation and talked behind the bar while Axel sat just behind her. He listened intently to their conversation. Jill planned a trip to Newport Rhode Island with Miguel to surprise friends, and she informed the bar manager about her pending departure. In the conversation, he learned Karen and James were the friends she was about to visit and Miguel was also traveling with her. All the members on Axel's hit list will be in Newport at the same time, Axel, too, made plans for Newport. As he returned to his room to book a flight to Providence, RI, he realized he was about to see more of the United States than he originally planned.

CHAPTER TWENTY-TWO

Karen heard from Miguel. He broke the news about their surprise visit to Newport for the 4th of July holiday in case Karen and James had other plans. Karen was excited to spend time with Jill since they hadn't seen each in a few weeks. It was a beautiful time of year to stroll the streets of downtown Newport while window shopping and Jill enjoyed it as much as Karen did. Karen thought it a perfect distraction to bring them to Devon Smith's party while they were there. Karen called Gloria to let her know she had company for the holiday. She posed her call as if she had to cancel plans due to her unexpected guests. Gloria's response was exactly what Karen hoped for, "You don't have to cancel, bring your company along, there will be hundreds of guests and a few more won't make a difference." Gloria was certain her guests would enjoy themselves even without knowing them because Devon went all out for the annual 4th of July gala, and everyone, friends and stranger alike, were almost assured a great time. Karen thanked her and looked forward to the big event even more so now that her close friends were also attending the party.

July 4th fell on a Saturday; Miguel and Jill arrived Thursday afternoon which gave the foursome plenty of time to catch up before the gala. Kevin chauffeured Karen and James to the small Providence airport and dropped them at the curb; Karen was so excited she was at least two paces ahead of James as they entered the terminal. Thankfully, she caught herself and slowed down to let him catch up to her. The two walked through the terminal to the arrivals screen hand in hand. Miguel and Jill's plane was due to touch down any minute. They agreed to meet in baggage claim and Karen and James were on their way there.

As the escalator descended into the baggage claim area, Karen watched the travelers carefully on the lookout for her friends. She beamed when they finally emerged on to the shiny steps. Karen hardly contained herself as the escalator ever so slowly brought them down one level, she wanted to yell out to them. Once they reach the bottom Jill and Karen embraced while James and Miguel shook hands. They made their way to the luggage belt and chatted away while they waited for their bags.

Axel descended into the arrival area on the same baggage claim escalator. He watched the group as they talked casually, and he took a seat on a bench on the opposite side of the baggage conveyer to get a closer look at the foursome. He arrived with one small travel bag but needed to pick up a hard cover case he checked on to the plane. He organized his maps and note pads while he watched the group of friends. His case rolled by on the carousel but he let it go by. He waited while Jill and Miguel identified their bags and moved away from the carousel before he took his bag. He made no eye contact with any of them while at the airport. He was anonymous.

James scooped up the bags from the carousel and they left the airport to load them into his sedan that was parked curbside. After he grabbed his case, Axel made his way to the rental counter and picked up a compact sized car. He rented a room for a week in Newport grumbling at the cost. During the peak summer months and, in this case, also a holiday weekend, he was lucky to find anything available. He found a room in town only because of a last-minute cancellation. It was $2500 for the week and he hoped he wasn't going to need a second week because the room was booked for the remainder of the summer. The house was located on a narrow side street but within a short walk to downtown shops and restaurants. Axel's rental was also ¾ of a mile away from Karen and James' condo. He called all over town trying to find something walking distance to their condo and lucked out after the cancellation popped up. He found the home easily and there was parking right out front. Once he had the key to his room, he dropped his bag on the queen size bed and left the small rental in search of supplies.

He came across a small grocer at the corner of Thames and Webster Streets where he purchased a few essentials he kept in the college-dorm sized refrigerator in the room. He ate in his room as much as possible to avoid small talk with a waitstaff but in reality, he simply preferred to be alone whenever possible.

After receiving Karen and James' address from Jorge, Axel spent a lot of time studying the local map where he memorized every street and restaurant on the waterfront. The Vanderbilt condominiums were easily found on the large map he spread out on the bed; all four targets were on the first-floor in condo #111. He retrieved a few slices of ham and a small block of cheese from the refrigerator. He ate slowly alternating bites of meat and cheese while he planned his route for the remainder of the day. After he ate, he surveyed the waterfront on foot.

Axel roamed the streets of downtown Newport marveling at the cobblestone artistry and the cleanliness of the busy tourist town. It was nothing like his hometown. He landed in Patti Cakes for an espresso and drank the steamy beverage while seated at a small iron table just outside the front door of the store and was casually glancing at a tourist map he found secured under the salt and pepper shaker on the table when Patti walked by. "How is your expresso?" Axle poured over the newly found map, oblivious to Patti's question but she had entered the store without stopping and quickly disappeared behind the counter to help a customer never giving the lone espresso drinker another thought.

After coffee, Axel strolled through town on foot and came upon the Vanderbilt condominiums when they appeared across from where he stood. The structure was built in the bay and an elaborate system of docks led to the residences. The docks were woven throughout the harbor, and Axel stepped up on the platform for a closer look. He followed along a path parallel to the shore where he studied the array of moored yachts that barely swayed in the tide. Along the way, he noticed two entrances to the Vanderbilt. He quickly deduced that he couldn't access the property because of the security system. There was a camera over each locked gate and access was granted by a security code and palm reader.

He lurked around the gate for as long as he could without drawing suspicion and decided the security system wasn't penetrable without more time and special tools, neither of which he had. To his surprise however, he saw directly into Karen and James' living room window from his vantage point. He never thought it he could get so close to his target this early in the process. He walked slowly along the dock and also realized he couldn't fire a weapon from the dock because there wasn't any privacy. Not only was the lack of privacy an issue, after he fired the weapon, he needed to slip into the crowd unnoticed and that couldn't happen either. The pedestrian docks were far too risky so he had to keep searching for a better spot.

A short distance away, on the commercial side of the moorage, he found an appropriate cover. There was also a small fishing boat that quietly motored behind the larger yachts, and he decided right then that a small boat was the perfect solution to his access problem. If he rented a fishing boat and sat in wait until he had his targets in sight, he could shoot them, and simply motor away quietly while hidden behind the yachts. There was movement everywhere in the busy harbor and in a small boat, he would blend in. Returning to his room, he flipped through the yellow pages in search of the nearest boat rental. He contacted three rental outfits and contracted three until he finally reached someone who had a boat available. He agreed to meet the owner and pick up the rental boat in the morning. He was one step closer to fulfilling the contract for Jorge Travares.

CHAPTER TWENTY-THREE

Friday July 3, Axel awoke before his 7:00 am alarm and wasted no time getting the day started. After a quick shower, he retrieved three hardboiled eggs and a cup of orange juice from his mini fridge. While he sat at the small kitchenette table, he alternated a bite of egg with a sip of juice in meticulous fashion. He located the boat rental company on the map and planned to pick up the rental by 10:00 am and he wanted to arrive no later than 9:55 am. He left his room at 9:00 am and returned to Patti's for an expresso. He overheard the pastry shop cashier's conversation about a 4th of July party at a mansion in town. Axel listened intently as the young girls carried on, it was clear, they wished they were invited. It sounded like a lavish affair, but he didn't pay much more attention to the chatter because he had to get the boat on time.

He completed the rental agreement, using one of his nine different sets of identifications, this time, he was posing as a traveler from Portugal. Axel secured the rental and loaded up the small fishing boat with a duffle bag that contained a riflescope, fruit and plenty of bottled water. He was wished a Happy 4th by the shop owner as he pulled away from the dock. Axel nodded and slowly motored away.

Instead of heading out into open water, he steered toward the inner harbor near the Vanderbilt where he staked out a proper spot to monitor James and Karen. The condo complex had a private waterway where homeowners moored their boats, but, though Axel wasn't inside the Vanderbilt's locked waterway, there were plenty of other places to hide within the crowded boat yard. He pulled in among some of the yachts along the docks and confirmed he wasn't seen by foot traffic. As he moved about unnoticed, he heard the chatter of people as they approached the locked gate to the residences. Karen, James, Miguel and Jill were together on the docks. James entered the security code and placed his hand onto the reader. The gate clicked open and the group proceeded to the condo. Axel sat in his small boat and watched them socialize inside their unit. He never heard them but saw them laughing and talking while he watched through one of their windows. He was in the perfect spot right where he was and wished he had his rifle with him not just the scope for it. The American holiday of July 4th was going to busy enough for him to move around unnoticed and he vowed to return to that very spot on Saturday to kill his targets.

CHAPTER TWENTY-FOUR

Jill and Miguel were glad they made the trip to Newport and they were all having a great time celebrating together. Unlike Miguel's or Jill's places in Florida, the Newport condo was within walking distance of the quaint downtown and all its activity. Karen never told Jill and Miguel she was currently working in Newport, but Jill knew Karen consulted with the FBI, and she moved there because of work. They may or may not assume she was working on the holiday weekend, but Karen was thankful neither Jill nor Miguel asked her anything about it. Her friends respected her privacy and their current lack of interest in her professional life made it easier for everyone that weekend.

When Saturday arrived, the four were in a festive mood. James made a huge breakfast and was really proud of his culinary achievement. It was heartwarming for Karen to watch her three favorite people as they chatted over breakfast. However, her thoughts drifted while she continued only half listening to their conversation about the food. She was thinking about tonight's party at Heavy D's. She wanted to slip inside his office while the security team was distracted by the hundreds of guests throughout the house. She hoped to have the chance to get inside his office unnoticed and will look for information that would help the taskforce knowing she was the only person who had direct contact with Heavy D and the only one who had close access to his personal office.

Heavy D hired college students to transport drugs from Columbia to the US and, even though the FBI hacked into his computer, they went through the system with a fine-tooth comb but there wasn't anything connecting him to the student transport ring. The team assumed Devon kept handwritten information somewhere in the office since his computer proved useless. If she found any information about Rebecca Jones, it made the risk worth it, and a huge plus for her personally. Rebecca hadn't been seen since her last trip to Columbia over spring break and her disappearance bugged the heck out of Karen. If she got caught in the office, she would say she needed a quiet place to make a phone call, but she was confident she could slip in and out unnoticed. James quietly gave Karen's arm a quick squeeze and she refocused her attention back to the breakfast conversation among her friends. They toasted the 4th of July holiday over orange juice.

They walked over to Devon Smith's party later that day and found his home even more impressive close up. When they reached the small private street, there were only 4 properties listed on the private property sign; Devon's entrance was just past the first curve on the left. They walked 300 yards up the stone paver driveway already lined with cars and found two members of a security team who flanked a giant black iron gate that swung open as the group approached. There were people in the driveway up ahead and the noise from the crowd grew louder as they neared the house. Karen stopped in the semi-circular driveway and took in the sheer size of the house. The valets parked cars along the entry way and the main road and kept the driveway out front clear for foot traffic to the house. Heavy D had good taste; the house was beautiful and fit perfectly into the New England setting, where its white trimmed gray exterior reeked of old-world charm and money. It certainly did not look like it could possibly belong to a drug dealer.

Sitting on about an acre of prime land, there were four distinct parts to the giant house. On the right, antique coach lights flanked the cedar doors of a two-car garage with a huge room over the top connected to the main part of the house. The garage flowed to the next structure where the main living areas were located. This section of the home was a three-story square structure with two long porches on the second and third levels. The final section of the mansion was another tall structure with round windows and a widows' walk surrounded by a third wrap around porch that afforded an ocean view from almost anywhere in the home. The house sat on a small parcel of land a short distance to the harbor and downtown shops. Karen guessed the house had a $5M price tag, if not more due to the location.

There was a flurry of activity in front of the house. Guests arrived on foot and valets swiftly parked cars. James escorted Karen by the arm as they made their way to the front door. As she stepped inside, Gloria appeared out of nowhere, "I'm so glad you made it, it's nice to see you again James" He flashed a huge smile, "It's nice to see you again too Gloria, these are our friends, Miguel and Jill." "Welcome to Newport, I'm happy you were able to join us. This is our 3rd annual party and we have a spectacular fireworks display lined up after dark!" They exchanged pleasantries and Gloria escorted them to the main living room where many of the guests gathered. As usual, Heavy D spared no expense and the waiters served champagne and appetizers to everyone in the room. Karen scanned the guests but didn't recognize anyone except for Gloria and her small crew of friends. Gloria was on the other side of the room as she tried, unsuccessfully, to get Heavy D's attention.

James was profiled in the Financial Times and Inc. Magazine, so the mayor recognized him immediately and pushed his way through the crowd to bend his ear. Karen was introduced to Mayor Thompson and Gloria was on her way over to their group with Heavy D in tow. "Karen, this is Devon – Devon, my friends Karen and James". Karen was first to extend a hand "pleased to meet you Devon, you have a beautiful home." James followed and the men made small talk with the Mayor.

Karen hadn't seen Devon since she was in her teens but the very sight of him reminded her of all the reasons why she hated him. She never flinched when she was introduced to him and there was no way he recognized her from their childhood, nor did he seem to care much about meeting her. Devon looked like a very wealthy and confident man with his perfectly straight white teeth, tailored pants, casual shirt, and Italian leather shoes. He was unadorned by any jewelry except for a tasteful fine watch.

Devon struck up a conversation with James about the Vanderbilt. As they discussed the merits of the property Devon mentioned that he would find it intrusive to live in a first-floor condo with the boats going in and out of the harbor so close to home. James assured him the condo wasn't as close to the waterway as it seemed, and most people were polite and didn't stare. Mayor Thompson eagerly chimed in and boasted about his role in getting the Vanderbilt constructed during his time in office. "It was quite a challenge to get that structure built in the first place. The locals thought their views of the harbor were spoiled forever but I assured them we wouldn't ruin the landscape. It took two years to finally get the zoning approved. You are living in an exclusive home James, and I suppose you have me to thank." "Thank you sir; we are very happy there." James tolerated the self-serving Mayor and actively listened as he continued talking about himself and his accomplishments in front of the small group.

Once darkness fell, the party goers were asked to find places on one of the many porches, the chairs set up in the driveway, or on the small lawn. It was time for the fireworks display that was set off in the harbor from a barge about three tenths of a mile away. As the crowd slowly moved outside, Karen found it an optimal time to sneak away to Heavy D's office. There was so much movement happening in the house, it was now or never. Gloria gave Karen a tour of the home shortly after they arrived and when they came upon Heavy D's office doors, they were locked but, with all the distractions currently in the house, Karen picked the lock and slipped inside the office without being seen.

Before she left, she asked James to find a spot on the upper deck and he saved her a chair before she slipped away. She kissed him on the cheek and headed straight to Heavy D's office. Hired hands continued escorting guests out of the house but due to the sheer number of partygoers it took a while before they all made their way outside. There had to be well over 100 people in attendance and no one noticed Karen as she lingered in front of the office doors with a small tool inside the lock. Once the door clicked and unlocked, she stepped inside easily.

Thankfully, Heavy D left a desk lamp on which made it easy to find her way around the office. He didn't have any file cabinets and the décor was sleek and ultra-modern, a bit over the top for her tastes, but somehow it still fit with the style of the rest of the house. His desk was a giant glass resting on a thin base with iron legs. There was a decorative iron cabinet next to the leather sofa that looked like it was used for storage. An animal pelt rug lay in front of the couch and, as she knelt on the rug, to look at the cabinet, she noticed the softness of the fur though she has no idea what animal gave their life for that rug. She reached for the cabinet hasp and thankfully, it was unlocked. There were 10 identical leather- bound journals stacked on a shelf inside.

Karen pulled out one of the journals and quickly scanned a few pages. There wasn't much helpful information inside the book. The notations looked like an old book-makers log with games, scores, and payments dating back many years. The next journal contained addresses and phone numbers, again not what she hoped to find. She didn't have a lot of time, but the next journal was more like the book she wanted. That book contained names, destinations, payments, and dates. The years dated back too far back for their current investigation but when Karen randomly pulled out the 6th book in the top row, she discovered a more recent time line. The book included first names only, with dates and payment amounts. There were random comments after each line, but only Heavy D understood the strange abbreviation system. One entry looked like it could be tied to Rebecca because of the destination and date, but there was no corresponding payment. Since Rebecca was missing, it might be noteworthy for the taskforce. It was the only link she found in the short time she had before someone might discover her in the office.

Even though Karen only had a few minutes to glance through the journals, she felt in her gut that Heavy D was connected to Rebecca's disappearance. She desperately wanted to prove Rebecca worked for him when she disappeared and the pages from the journal were the only evidence she had thus far. The taskforce had proof that Rebecca went away on spring break in March and the name and destination in the logbook coincided with that trip. There were other similar notations during that same week suggesting there was a link between the other drug smuggling students and those notes. The taskforce had the names of the accomplices and if their first names matched up to the entries in the journal, it was the first time they had evidence in writing. It wasn't enough to convict him yet, but it was a solid start.

Heavy D had a small copier in the office, and Karen quickly made copies of the important pages and put the book back in proper order on the shelf in the cabinet. She folded the copies and stuffed them into her small purse. After a quick scan of the office to make sure she left it the way she found it, she tousled the nape of the animal rug to remove any knee imprints before she left. She thought she heard a glass break and slipped through the doors unnoticed to join James on the porch.

CHAPTER TWENTY-FIVE

Karen paused outside the door of Heavy D's office, her mind wandering to Rebecca Jones. How did a young woman disappear without a trace and, even worse, apparently, no one cared that she was missing? Rebecca weighed heavily on her mind until she was jolted out of her thoughts by a woman screaming somewhere in the house. Karen was startled when a waiter come towards her at a full run. "What's going on?" He didn't stop to answer but he yelled as he continued down the hallway, "there was a shooting!" Karen's heart was pounding. She had to get to James. She tore down the hallway where she found a crowd gathered around someone on the floor in the living room. Panicked voices echoed throughout the room shrieking, "Call 911."

The music finally cut off and everyone in the house was frantic. Karen found James on the other side of the living room next to Heavy D and she pushed through the crowd to get to him. The group of onlookers were frozen in place and Karen continued pushing through the crowd until she saw what happened. She felt like she ran in slow motion while she slogged her way over to James.

Before she reached him however, she stopped dead in her tracks. Miguel was on the floor with cradled Jill in his arms. She wasn't moving and it hit Karen like a ton of bricks that Jill was shot. But how? Why? There was an ever-growing pool of blood that surrounded them. It looked like half of Jill's head was caved in, and Jill and Miguel were equally covered in blood. Karen wasn't sure if Miguel was also shot. She finally pushed through and squatted down next to Miguel on the floor. "Are you okay?" "I'm fine - please help Jill", he said through tearful eyes. Karen carefully helped Miguel lay her flat on the floor and began performing CPR. She was determined to keep Jill alive until the paramedics arrived. Jill was a friend and sister all wrapped in the same person and Karen promised to save her even though it was hard to think clearly during the chaos in the room. Karen had no idea yet what happened but continued working on Jill.

Gloria stood close by watching Karen, also in shock. It seemed like an eternity for the ambulance to arrive while Karen continued to push on Jill's chest. It was impossible for her to hold back her tears any longer. She cried as she begged Jill to stay with her. It felt like hours, but she heard the faint sound of the sirens grew louder as they neared and prayed to God he spared her friend. As the ambulance crew raced into the house, they assured her they were ready to take over. Karen backed away from Jill but stood close by shaking from head to toe as the medical team worked. They took Jill's vital signs, carefully put her on a backboard, and loaded her on to the stretcher. They never rushed her out of the house and Karen was afraid they already lost her. She tried to keep some shred of optimism, but it was difficult to stay positive while Jill's lifeless body was on the gurney in front of her. The EMT squeezed the plastic air bag that filled Jill's lungs with oxygen and the team wheeled her outside.

Miguel rode to the hospital in the back of the ambulance and Karen promised to meet him there after she spoke to the police. Gloria was visibly shaken and Heavy D had a few trusted employees who surrounded him when the trouble started. He spoke heatedly to one of his men but Karen never heard what he said. Everything was a blur and all she heard was a low humming noise that echoed in her head. The party guests scrambled to get out of the house and the local police tried to stop them from leaving the scene. They wanted everyone back inside for questioning.

Four police cars squeezed into the remaining space in the driveway in front of the house. There were three local cruisers and one car belonged to the police detective. Detective Chuck Workman who had a brief talk with the officers at the scene before they spread out through the house and on to the grounds. He asked Devon's employees to lock the iron gates until the police were able to question all the guests. Heavy D wasn't pleased by their suggestion because he didn't want his guest inconvenienced but he finally gave in. The officers did their best to keep the remaining guests inside until they were questioned but it is a difficult task. A third officer corralled the guests outside and asked them to please return to the house.

Two of the officers began interviewing guests in the house while the other officers calmed the tense crowd and promised everyone a swift departure. Detective Workman approached Heavy D.

"Mr. Smith, I'm Detective Workman from the Newport Police Department. I'd like to find out what happened tonight. How do you know the victim?"

"I don't know her - she came with friends of my girlfriend"

"Do you know if anyone at the party may have wanted to hurt her"?

"I told you; I don't know her. I have no idea why anyone would want to hurt her. Talk to her friends." Heavy D pointed toward James and Karen. As Detective Workman made note that Devon Smith didn't know the victim, his cell phone rang.

"Mr. Smith, Jill Freeman is dead."

Karen was close enough to hear their conversation and fell to her knees when she heard the words. Jill was dead. She didn't know whether to go to the hospital, go home, or remain there on the floor crying. James lifted her up and held her while she made a half-hearted attempt to compose herself. She found the closest restroom, wiped her eyes, and stood quietly for a moment while she tried to make sense of the events. As she stared at her reflection in the mirror, it was impossible to comprehend what just happened. She splashed cold water on her face and held the towel over her eyes for an extra few seconds before she returned to the living room. She hoped it was a bad dream but when she saw the blood-stained floor, she fought back tears all over again. The police learned nothing from the guests at the party. No one saw or heard anything. In fact, few guests even noticed Jill that night. Karen and James left the house devastated.

CHAPTER TWENTY-SIX

In the harbor aboard the small rented fishing boat, Axel shifted positions from one seat to the other as he reloaded the rifle. He aimed perfectly, and as planned, Jill was dead first. He moved on to his next target, James Caulfield III. Axel peered through the rifle scope until he found James standing next to a tall black man. Unmoved by the police presence at the house, Axel regained his balance after a passing boat caused a slight ripple in the calm water. He placed the rifle into position and watched the panicked crowd inside the house through the scope. He didn't have a clear shot at James due to the commotion, but he patiently waited for his next victim to come back into view.

Axel watched partygoers flee from the house, as the lights from the police cars flickered in the night sky. The guests scurried toward their cars stunned by the gunshots. There was a lot of commotion in and around the house while Axel remained anonymous in his rental boat in the busy harbor. He steadied the rifle, checked his sights one last time, and squeezed the trigger. He never moved his eye from the scope until James fell against the wall. Axel calmly arose from his squatting position, carefully removed the scope from his long-range Remington 700 rifle and placed it back in its case. He dismantled the rest of the rifle and placed each piece carefully into their designated foam indents in the case. He placed the case under the seat of the boat and was on the move. Ever so slowly he followed along behind the traffic leaving the harbor and exited unnoticed. It was 8:30 pm, more than an hour after sunset. The town fireworks display was beginning at 9:10 pm and there was a lot more traffic in the harbor. Axel moved around the harbor virtually invisible in the dark, confident he was unnoticed due to all the extra traffic. He motored quietly to the next public dock, moored the boat in his paid space, and hopped up on the dock carrying a duffle bag with the gun case tucked inside. He casually tossed the bag over his shoulder and walked back to his room.

Detective Workman ran to James as he fell against the wall into a seated position. He had blood on his shoulder but seemed to be okay otherwise. Karen was on her way back from the bathroom when she saw James fall. The Detective called for another ambulance and whoever was left in the house ran out in shear panic. The police rushed the remaining guests out now that a second person was shot. The house was a war zone. It was as if the town was under siege as Karen raced to James. The few people too afraid to go outside hid from the windows and hit the floor. Even Heavy D squatted down out of sight and pulled Gloria down with him for fear the shooter wasn't done.

When he felt safe enough to stand, Devon Smith was angry, steaming mad was more like it. Someone ruined his party and he assumed the shooter was out for him since he was near Jill when she was shot, and he stood next to James when he was shot. Karen overheard him order his security manager to "find him now." Gloria was by his side while Karen applied a towel to James's shoulder while they waited for the ambulance. James assured her he was okay, "the bullet grazed my shoulder and I will be fine, please stop fussing over me." Nothing made sense that night. Jill was murdered and now James was shot. Was the shooter trying to kill Heavy D in his own home in front of hundreds of witnesses, or was the shooter after someone else? She wondered if her past was coming back to haunt her. Her head spun and she was dizzy.

Detective Workman pulled the .308 caliber bullet that grazed James' shoulder out of the wall with a pair of pliers, placed it in an evidence bag, and asked an officer to take it to the car for safe keeping. James insisted he didn't need an ambulance and didn't want to go to the hospital but agreed to go to be with Miguel. Karen didn't let him off the hook, "you are going in the ambulance, and I'm going with you. You might need stitches and I want you checked out, no arguments." A second ambulance arrived at the Smith residence and James was loaded inside. Karen rode with him and tried to think of comforting words for Miguel when they saw him. She teared up again when she thought about Jill but she was also relieved James was okay. She held his hand tightly and stared at his handsome face during the ride to the hospital.

Newport Hospital was a quick 10-minute trip while the lights and sirens blared. The Emergency room physician assured them that after a few stitches, James was going to be fine. The bullet only grazed his shoulder and there wasn't any significant damage. He was very lucky the bullet didn't rip his shoulder apart. As James sat on the thin bed in the ER with his shirt off, Karen stared at his muscular chest. He caught her looking, "Karen, I'm fine, please stop worrying."

"I'm not worried, but I am relieved you are okay, and I need to find Miguel. I promised him we would bring him home. Do you mind if I skip out to find him while they finish up with you?"

"Go find him, I'll call Kevin to come get us and wait here for you."

She kissed him, wiped her tears, and took a deep breath before she opened the door.

One of the ER nurses showed Karen to an office Miguel used to call Jill's parents in private. The door opened and there sat Miguel, defeated and slumped over in the chair with this head in his hands. He lifted his head when Karen entered the room and it was obvious his eyes were swollen and red. She rushed to him and flooded his shoulder with tears as they cried together.

He broke the silence, "who could have done this? Do you know?"

"I have no idea, I don't think anyone was after Jill, I think she was in the wrong place at the wrong time and the shooter was after someone else."

"Who?" Miguel was visibly frustrated, "the host of the party? Did he put Jill in danger?"

"Miguel, I'm so sorry. I promise you I will find out who did this. He started toward the door as Karen talked. "James is at the hospital too, the gunman fired again, and he was hit in the shoulder." Miguel stopped in his tracks. "He will be fine. He only needed a few stitches and he is waiting for us in the emergency room. He called his driver before I came to find you, and I'm sure he is outside by now. If there are police or reporters in the emergency room looking for you, we are not stopping to talk to anyone, I want to get you out of here."

James and Miguel embraced briefly when they saw each other and the three headed for the exit doors. Just as the emergency room doors swooshed open, Detective Workman was on his way in. James held up his hand, "not tonight, we've had enough" and they continued to the car where Kevin waited with an open door. Detective Workman yelled from the doorway, "I will be by tomorrow then, good night."

The three friends rode back to the condo together. Miguel assured them he didn't need help with the funeral and would be in touch once the arrangements were made. Karen tried to keep up with the conversation, but she was emotionally drained. She helped Miguel get settled in the guest room, and James promised his private jet to take him back to Florida in the morning whenever he wanted to leave. By the time Karen got to their bedroom, the only thing she longed for was sleep. James waited for her and she curled up next to him. He propped himself atop the pillows and looked down on her. "I'm so thankful you weren't hurt. I don't know what I would do without you but I want to talk. You just lost your closest friends, and I was shot. Is your work with the FBI worth all of this?" She didn't have the energy to argue with him; she adjusted her head on his good shoulder and promised to think about it. She had tortured dreams most of the night while she tried to piece the chaos together. Even in her dreams, she lost track of her thoughts, and tossed and turned all night.

CHAPTER TWENTY-SEVEN

As promised, Detective Workman knocked on the condo door at 9:30 am.

"Good morning Ms. Anderson, I have a few questions for you if this is a good time?"

"It's fine, come in." She guided the detective to the kitchen where they sat at the island. She offered coffee but he held up his hand and wanting to get right to work.

"How well do you know Devon Smith?"

"I don't know him, I am friends with Gloria. We met earlier this summer and became friends. She invited us to the party and we were introduced to Devon Smith for the first time that night."

"Did Jill Freeman know Devon Smith?"

When he mentioned Jill in the same sentence with Heavy D, it stabbed at her heart. She never mentioned her association with the FBI. She didn't know if she could trust the detective, so she kept her identity to herself until she had more time to assess the situation.

"NO, Jill didn't know any of them! I brought Jill and Miguel along as my guests and I will never forgive myself for inviting them. I didn't know anyone except for the host, and I don't mean to be rude but we're rehashing the same questions you asked last night. Nothing has changed since we last spoke and we have a busy morning. Miguel is traveling to Florida today and we need to get him to the airport."

"I know it seems like I'm asking the same questions over again, but I need to make sure you didn't remember anything new after a night's rest".

"I assure you Detective, the last thing I did last night was rest. If there isn't anything else, I will show you out."

Detective Workman wasn't ready to leave but James insisted they told him everything they knew and they needed some privacy before Miguel's departure. Detective Workman promised to leave once he closed the loop with Miguel. The Detective asked him the same questions he asked Karen and even though he was exhausted, Miguel cooperated. Thankfully the Detective left when they finished talking.

Detective Workman pieced the case together and the evidence pointed towards an attempt on Devon Smith's life, it was the most logical conclusion. Devon believed he was a pillar in the community, but his police record painted a different picture. He was arrested for drug trafficking twice although the charges never stuck. The witnesses in two separate cases conveniently disappeared, or "forgot" how they knew Devon Smith a.k.a. Heavy D so the police never believed his good Samaritan persona.

Detective Workman's theory was that someone had a grudge and shot at Devon Smith twice during the party. The shooter may not have been a professional marksman for hire, because he, or she, missed him, hitting two innocent bystanders instead. It was difficult to determine where the shooter was located, he could have hidden anywhere in the small wooded area across from the Smith house. The security guards posted at the gate never saw anyone on foot nor did a car pass by close enough to the property to take aim at anyone inside. They never saw a gun flash and never left their posts. They told the truth, and Detective Workman ruled out the security staff. Technically, the gunman could have been up to a mile away from the house based on the munitions used, but it meant he had to be an exceptional marksman if he was confident enough to take aim from that distance. Since Devon wasn't shot, the detective focused his attention closer to home.

The detective ruled nothing out this early in the investigation and while he had his own assumptions, he didn't have enough information yet. He had to vet the possibility that the shooter was in fact further away due to the caliber bullet retrieved at the scene. That particular bullet was fired from a long-range rifle, meaning the shooter could have been anywhere in the harbor since it was at least a mile away from the house. While unlikely, it was worth investigating further.

Officers fanned out on the docks to question anyone who worked on the 4ᵗʰ of July. The officers scoured the area and spoke to any workers and deckhands they came across, but the stories were all the same. No one saw anything suspicious or provided any new leads. There was so much additional traffic in the harbor because of the holiday, it would have been difficult for anyone to pinpoint the sound of gunshots because of all the fireworks being set off on the personal crafts. Additionally, no one saw anyone flee the area around the time of the shooting that evening. There were parties on boats and a lot of out of town guests with yachts moored close by so it was hard to discern who was a local and who wasn't. The police had no further information to support a shooter in the small bay near the Smith house and nothing looked out of place to those questioned. Thus far, the detective had very little to go on and no suspect.

Detective Workman went over the witness list from the party a few more times to see if he missed anything, then made an appointment to speak with Devon Smith for a second time. The Detective was shown through the Iron Gate after the security guard called the house and Gloria met him at the front door.

"Please come in Detective, Devon will meet you in the sunroom. I'll let him know you are here." The Detective walked by the living room and noticed the carpet was already replaced. After the shooting, the police needed a small section of rug as evidence and Devon instructed them to take the entire carpet knowing it was useless with a missing piece. It appeared Devon was more upset about the loss of his expensive carpet than the fact that someone was murdered in his house. The Detective waited patiently for almost ten minutes before Devon made his way to the sunroom.

The men shook hands and sat in two leather-tufted armchairs. They were as opposite as two men could be. Detective Workman saw Devon as a slick salesman while Devon treated the detective like a rookie police officer. It wasn't long before they were offered coffee by one of the staffers.

"Mr. Smith, now that you've had some time to think since the shooting, do you know of anyone who might want to hurt you?"

Devon slyly smiled, "Detective, I'm sure a lot of people want me dead. I'm a wealthy black man living in an old money, predominantly white, town."

"Have you been threatened? Have you had any arguments recently with anyone in particular?"

"Detective, you have a job to do and I appreciate that but as I told you before, I don't know anyone who would be brazen enough to shoot me in my own home in front of hundreds of witnesses. It was embarrassing, and I want to know who had the balls to do it."

"You were embarrassed?" the Detective tried not to sound as surprised as he felt.

"I have a lot of respect in this town and bullets raining down on my party is quite simply - embarrassing. I have my men looking for the shooter and if we find him before you do, I'm not going to call you. I have work to do, are we done?"

Detective Workman rose and was shown to the door by a staffer. He sat in his car and took a long look at the house. It looked pristine, no broken glass anywhere. It was almost as if the events from the party were erased and life moved on. The Detective had a renewed sense of urgency to find the shooter before Heavy D did.

CHAPTER TWENTY-EIGHT

Karen had a conversation with Mr. & Mrs. Freeman earlier in the day long before Detective Workman arrived with more questions. That call reminded her why Freeman's were amazing parents. While Karen felt responsible for Jill's death because she invited her to the party, Jill's parents felt differently. They never blamed Karen and reassured her she would always be their adopted daughter and Jill's best friend. The Freeman's were proud parents. They spent at least 30 minutes on the phone with Karen while they boasted about how special Jill was and never shed a tear. They knew a lot about their daughter as an adult. They knew how successful she was because she worked hard and earned the respect of her peers. Jill never expected anyone to do more than she would do and all of her employees at the Excelsor Polo Club held her in high regard for it. She was a hands-on manager and no job was beneath her. If a guest or member needed help, she was there to lend a hand. The Freemans knew their daughter so well and Karen marveled at their close relationship.

Miguel and the Freeman's jointly planned the funeral to take place in Florida with dinner served at Jill's club after the services. Miguel promised to cover the cost of the dinner and, knowing how much he loved her, he spared no expense. The Freeman's wanted to bury their daughters' ashes in a special sanctuary befitting Jill. James offered to take care of all the arrangements, but Miguel wanted to handle it along with Jill's parents. Karen was thankful Miguel had the distraction. Keeping busy was what he needed to keep his mind off his grief.

Miguel, James and Karen shared a tearful goodbye when it was time for Miguel to leave. They had a quiet ride to the airport and when they reached the terminal, Karen got out first and gave Miguel another big bear hug. "Once the arrangements are made, we be will there with you and please call me if there is anything I can do to help. We are here for you and I mean it – anything." He hugged her tightly in return and leaned his head into the car, "Thanks for the plane back to Florida James, I owe you one." James tapped on Miguel's shoulder, "the pilot will meet you once you're through security, safe travels my friend."

The morning paper leaned against the door of Axel's room and fell on his foot when he opened it. The front page was filled with the events that occurred at the Smith's 4th of July party and he was dismayed to read that James was still alive. He saw him drop and was certain he killed him. It was the first time he missed a target. The more he read about the subtle injury James received to his shoulder, the more he ruminated over his failure. He chastised himself because he should have stayed in the harbor until it was confirmed that James was dead. He didn't complete the mission; he was not a soldier.

Axel phoned Jorge to report in. Jill was dead but James was still alive, but not for long. Axel was careful when he spoke to Jorge and used hunting terminology as a ruse in case anyone heard him through the paper-thin walls. "I had a perfect place to shoot the huge buck and had two in my sights. I missed the second one. I don't know what happened". Jorge was pleased Axel carried out the contract so quickly, "one confirmed kill is a good start. I haven't lost faith in you Axel. James, Miguel and Karen will meet their fates, I trust in you so be patient."

Jorge wasn't upset by the call and Axel got back to business. James was next and Axel wasn't going to miss the second time. He reviewed the local map one more to find a new hiding place along the waterfront. Since Karen and James' condo faced the docks, Axel thought he could sneak in quietly between the boats unnoticed by anyone inside the dwelling. He wanted to kill them both and return home, but he had to follow the orders given and that meant James had to die before Karen. More specifically, Axel had to kill James in front of Karen because that's what Jorge wanted and paid for. Jorge, who was consumed by hatred, longed for revenge, and wanted Karen to watch her lover die right before her eyes.

CHAPTER TWENTY-NINE

Karen and Mark hadn't spoken in quite some time and she owed him a call after all that happened at Heavy D's party. His words were comforting, "I'm really sorry for your loss. This was not your fault. You couldn't have predicted someone would take a shot at Heavy D while you were there. I read about the shooting in the paper and we did a quick check to see if anyone on our radar looked like an obvious suspect. Unfortunately, no one was in the area at the time. Of course, anyone could have hired someone to kill Heavy D but we don't have any leads for you. I will let you know if we come up with something, but we aren't investigating the shooting, we are leaving that to the locals as you probably already assumed." Karen wasn't thrilled with the news, but she knew the shooting was ultimately a local matter. At least Detective Workman kept searching for the person who took the life of her dear friend. She promised full attention on the assignment but had to attend the funeral in Florida. "No problem Karen, maybe Heavy D will let something slip now that he is convinced someone is trying to kill him. You can catch up with Gloria when you're back."

Karen emerged from her office after the call still emotionally drained. When she entered the kitchen, James was sitting on a stool at the island.

"I made you a latte, would you like anything to eat?"

"No thanks, coffee is fine."

"Karen, I realize you are hurting but I am not avoiding this conversation any longer. I want to go back to Florida with you and I'm asking you to leave the task force behind. I don't understand why you want to put yourself in harms-way on purpose."

"For God's sake James, you know I can't predict what's going to happen when I'm in the field and I'm not putting myself in harms-way on purpose."

"You know what I mean, getting to know Gloria to gather information was one thing, but you just lost your closest friend, and I was shot in the process. Are you next? Is that what it will take?"

"We've had this conversation before; you know I'm not quitting."

"Do you need more excitement? Is that it? Are you bored?"

"Don't be ridiculous, you knew I worked for the FBI when I met you. It's who I am and if I have a chance to make the world a safer place, I'm going to do it."

"I don't want to lose you and I don't want to worry every time you leave the house."

"I love you for worrying about me, but I've been taking care of myself for a long time and I'm a lot tougher than you think. How about we bring our coffee to our room and take a little morning "nap"?"

"You can't change the subject with sex although I like the way you think" He softened and wrapped his arms around her. Karen was relieved the conversation was over for now.

Karen spent the rest of the day writing a eulogy for Jill. She was proud of their friendship the more she recalled their many outings together. They were fiercely independent women but sought advice from each another because of the trust between them. James planned a morning flight for them to attend the funeral. Karen wasn't looking forward to the service but also wouldn't miss it for anything in the world.

Although Karen and James were inside the condo all day, they remained in their separate offices. Karen appreciated him leaving her alone with her thoughts. At almost 4:00 pm, she found him still working in his office and sat in front of him on his desk while he completed a call. She had her feet on top of his thighs, and he had a sly grin while he continued talking. She softly dug her toes into his waist, and he coyly nodded that it was okay to continue. Before his call ended, her clothes were off and she had him half undressed. He only half listened to the caller and when she heard the phone click off; they made love on the couch in his office. They laid in each other's arms, Karen energized by their afternoon sexual escapade while James nodded on and off.

After a short rest, Karen leaped up off the couch and announced, "I'm starved, let's get something to eat. Last one in the shower pays for dinner." She tore off like a shot with James was right behind her. He was an amazing man. He was on the phone discussing a deal worth millions of dollars, but he allowed himself to be distracted and now raced her to the shower. Karen was an incredibly lucky woman and for the first time since the shooting, she was playful, laughing, and present.

CHAPTER THIRTY

James and Karen arrived at the Boca Raton Airport at 11:00 am and easily found the transportation Kevin arranged to bring them to the beach house. Kevin stayed behind awaiting their return to Newport after the funeral. Even though it was a sad reason to be back in Florida, it was good for them to see the house and the ocean behind it. James was on the back deck looking out over the water while Karen remained inside talking with Miguel about the funeral arrangements.

She joined James on the deck and filled him in on the arrangements. "They aren't planning a wake. There is a memorial service tomorrow morning at St. Jude's Church at 11:00, then a luncheon at the Club." They leaned on the deck rail while the gentle waves washed ashore, agreeing to attend the private internment service at the mausoleum with the Freemans before they met the guests at the club.

When Karen woke the next day, a wave of sadness rushed over because she had to say goodbye to her closest friend in a few hours. James was attentive and supportive all morning. They arrived at the church at 10:15 am to find Miguel already seated inside. A huge portrait of Jill was on a table near the altar and there were flowers everywhere. The Freeman's hadn't arrived yet so Miguel and Karen got to spend a few quiet minutes alone. He looked like he hadn't slept much and asked her to speak on Jill's behalf. Since Karen had worked on a eulogy for the past few days, she was happy to do it.

The funeral mass was touching. Karen shared favorite memories of Jill and Mr. Freeman also spoke about his daughter. It was surprising he could talk about Jill without collapsing when the loss was still so fresh, but there he was, proudly boasting about his beloved daughter. There wasn't a dry eye in the church.

Jill had many more friends than Karen realized and, after listening to the stories from her many friends and relatives, she wished she knew Jill even longer than she did. The family proceeded to the cemetery for a private interment service while the other guest went to the club; Jill's ashes were placed in a vault rather than in the ground. The rotunda, designed to hold the ashes of those who preferred cremation over full burials, was a majestic building centrally located in the heart of the cemetery. They parked outside the round structure and James held Karen's hand tightly as they walked inside the building. They followed the Freeman's to Jill's vault and there was a beautiful saying carved on the metal door. It read, "Life's journey has been all the better for you being in it, our dear Jill." Karen nodded after she read the inscription in acknowledgment that Jill touched her life in such a meaningful way also. Mrs. Freeman placed the brass urn inside the vault and slowly closed and locked the metal door. Miguel placed his hand on the vault and spent a few minutes alone with his thoughts before the group proceeded to the Excelsor for the Celebration of Life gathering to honor Jill.

The Club was packed. Most of the attendees from the church were there as well as numerous employees from the Club. Jill would have loved the party. It wasn't overdone and the food and wine choices were exquisite. Miguel did a fabulous job selecting all the things he thought Jill would have liked, and while it was a somber event, the guests loosened up as time passed and there was occasional laughter around the room. Mr. and Mrs. Freeman sat with James, Miguel and Karen, and enjoyed talking about Jill as a little girl. It was clear they were comforted by her friends during their difficult time.

The festivities ended around 7:00 pm and Karen looked forward to getting back home to be alone with James. He was so supportive, she wanted nothing more than to lie in his arms while she drifted off to a peaceful nights' rest after their emotional day. Miguel opted to remain at the club a bit longer. He had a ride home, so they left after sharing hugs all around. James put his arm around Karen in the car and she felt a little less sad. He brushed the hair away from her face and said, "We've been through a lot together and I want to get you home and put you to bed. We will move past our sorrow and I promise you, our lives will slow down a little."

Karen knew what he meant by slowing down but didn't want to talk about work or his desire for her to quit working with the FBI. She was too worn out for a long conversation. Instead, she closed her eyes and snuggled in closer to him for the remainder of the ride home. She was exhausted and longed for the comfort of their bed.

The next day Karen was well rested, in fact, it was the most rested she felt in a long time and was raring to get outside for some fresh air. She slid into nylon running pants with a matching top and James promised breakfast by the time she returned. She took a quick 3-mile run along the shore and realized she was slightly out of shape by the time she reached the top of the stairs back at the house. She stretched on the back deck and smelled the aroma of fried bacon that emanated from the house. Her stomach growled and she put off a hot shower until after their long leisurely breakfast was over.

She walked into the kitchen to find that James had a wonderful spread laid out as he handed her coffee. "I love the way you spoil me". "It's my job to spoil you." She kissed him and slid into her seat. She was famished and forced herself to slow down so she could eat like a respectable woman. They made small talk for the first 15 minutes or so and then she suggested they return to Newport the next morning. She was taken back when James' responded, "I'm not returning with you." She could have fallen off her chair. "What? Do you need more time at the house? Do you have work to do? I can put off my return for a few more days if you need the time?"
"It's not about my work Karen, it's about yours. I can't go back to Newport now. There is a ticking time bomb waiting to blow every time you leave the house. You received a pretty strong warning and you're ignoring it."
She was defeated. "I don't know what to say, you asked me to quit a job I love and I already told you I'm not going to do that. I wish you would try and support me rather than control me."

Karen pushed the chair back from the table, dropped her napkin on top of her plate, and left the kitchen. She was trapped. Even though the house was huge, she couldn't get far enough away from him and their conversation at that moment. He hurt her feelings more than he knew. She wanted to change nothing about him but now he wanted to change her and it wasn't fair. She had nothing left to discuss. She wasn't quitting her job and while the thought of returning to Newport without him was devastating, it was what she had to do.

"If you want me to stay someplace other than the condo let me know. The FBI can set me up with an apartment."

"Don't be ridiculous. I bought the condo for us; it's as much yours as it is mine. Don't you want to talk about this?"

"There is nothing to talk about, you want me to stay here and be something I'm not. What else is there to say?" Karen went into the bedroom, showered and pondered her next move while James stayed behind in the kitchen. They kept away from each other for the rest of the day.

CHAPTER THIRTY-ONE

The next morning Karen was dismayed when Kevin returned to Florida since that meant James was staying put, just as he said he was going to do. Karen arranged travel to Newport on a commercial flight and Kevin offered to drive her to the airport rather than a taxi or livery service. She eventually gave in and accepted his offer. Being too hurt to cry, she didn't feel much like talking to Kevin during the ride either. He cautiously glanced at her from the rear-view mirror and sensed something wasn't right, but he knew better than to say anything. She flew out of the main airport in Orlando because, even though James had offered the use of his jet, she was too stubborn to accept that offer. She sat in the sedan for almost an hour without a word between her and Kevin. Just before they pulled into the Delta departure lane, he finally broke the silence, "I hope James joins you again soon, have a safe trip Karen." She thanked him but didn't offer anything more in response. James was a private man and Kevin needn't not be privy to their personal strife. He was James' employee after all and not a close friend.

As she sat on the plane, she rehashed their morning argument. She was lucky to have him in her life, but she wasn't having the same disagreement over and over. Sadly, if he won't come to terms with her career, she can't continue sharing her life with him. She hadn't closed the door just yet and remained only mildly hopeful James will have a change of heart. She was flattered that Mark asked her to work with FBI after she resigned years earlier and won't give it up for James or anyone. As the plane touched down, she realized she slept off and on because the two-hour flight went by quickly.

Once settled in at the condo, Karen called Gloria to meet for coffee. To her surprise, Gloria insisted they meet at Heavy D's house instead of Patti's. Gloria was under close watch since the shooting and she never ventured too far off the property. It was an odd feeling going back to there after all that happened, and Karen wasn't excited about it. While Karen would have preferred the coffee shop, she went to Heavy Ds house because she needed an update, and Gloria was the closest source for information. Since they still assumed Heavy D was the target, Gloria was well informed on the investigation.

It was less humid, the sun beamed with a slight breeze, and Karen walked the half mile to meet Gloria. When she arrived at the entry of Heavy D's, the guard recognized her, opened the heavy steel gate, and welcomed her in without being prompted for ID. Gloria waited at the door when Karen neared the front of the house, "it's so good to see you! I hope you are holding up okay. Did you get the flowers we sent?" "The flowers were beautiful, everyone noticed them, thank you both."

"Come in, come in, it will be nice to get caught up, it's been a few weeks since we had any time together."

While it was odd being back in the house, Karen was comforted by Gloria's embrace, and both women were genuinely happy to see each other. They sat in the library rather than the living room, and coffee was served with four of Patti's pastries. Karen hadn't seen Patti in a long time and missed her handmade delights.

"Are you staying with Devon now?"

"I am, after the shooting he was afraid I might be targeted and, until we figure out who is after him, he prefers that Markis and I remain close by."

"Does he have any idea who might want to hurt him?"

"None, but as he says, it could be anyone with grudge against him and he wasn't taking chances with our lives."

Gloria had so much faith and trust in Heavy D, she will be deeply devastated when she learns the truth about him and his drug empire. Karen secretly wished she could just tell her now. The ladies chatted for an hour and Karen fibbed that James was on a business trip and won't return to Newport for a few more weeks. She couldn't bear to tell Gloria the truth because she hadn't really accepted it yet herself. Gloria understood what it was like to be alone and they agreed to meet again at Patti's. Patti had a lot of questions about the shooting and neither Gloria nor Karen had talked with her since the events unfolded.

Karen wandered through town before she returned home, and Axel spotted her as she walked the docks towards the condo. He hadn't known how long she would be away for the funeral. James wasn't with her but Axel had watched their activities long enough to know they sometimes went in and out alone and James was likely somewhere nearby. He rented another room over the small family grocery store on Mann Avenue and only having three days left on that rental, he had to move fast if he was going to complete the contracted hits for Jorge. The clocked ticked on Axel's rental while time also ticked away for James and Karen. He followed her at a safe distance until she went inside the condo and was ready to return after dark.

CHAPTER THIRTY-TWO

The condo seemed a lot bigger without James, it was too quiet. She imagined what he was doing. They hadn't talked since she left Florida and they never went a full day without speaking. She hemmed and hawed about calling him; she wasn't even sure why she waited so long to call because she wanted to hear his voice. She paced around the kitchen island talking to herself, as she decided what to do - call or not call. She didn't want him to think she caved on her principles, but then again, she hated for him to think she didn't care. Oh, for Pete's sake, she told herself, just call him!

She searched for the kitchen for her phone until she found it in the office on the desk right where she left it. She selected her favorites list and jumped when the phone rang. It was James!

"I can't believe you called. I just picked up the phone to call you!"

"I'm sorry. I hate the thought of losing you to some crazed maniac and I had to try one last time to get you out of harms-way but you're right, I need to support you rather than control you."

"James, I don't want....."

"Don't say another word, I have no right to ask you to stop working and I will never do it again. I'd like to come home."

"You are home, I'm the one who is away"

"Home is where you are Karen, not here in Florida, I will fly up tomorrow if you want me to."

"Yes! Of course, I want you here!"

"I love you and can't wait to see you."

To say she was relieved was an understatement.

She hung up the phone and let out a quick squeal of delight, but mostly felt a huge sense of relief. The man she loved was due back by her side while she was able to remain in a job she loved. It was almost too good to be true and she was afraid to count her blessings for fear she would jinx herself! She was happy and vowed to demonstrate her deep love and affection for him as often as she could. She never wanted him to wonder how she felt about him, and even more important, she never wanted to experience an impasse like that again.

James and Kevin flew into T.F. Green airport in Providence at 10:15 am. Once they arrived at the condo, Karen and James spent the remainder of the day in bed and took full advantage of "make-up" sex after their disagreement. It was clear neither of them wanted to be apart from the other. They hated to leave the comfort of the bedroom but when late afternoon hit, they were famished. A steamy shower together was just what they needed and under the hot water spray, they decided on Uncle Tony's for dinner.

They walked arm and arm across the docks onto the cobblestones of the downtown streets flirting along the way. Uncle Tony's was a favorite and they requested a corner table outside. The wait staff whispered to each other as the couple walked through the restaurant; no doubt they remembered their generous tips, and it warranted a coin-toss to see who serviced their table. Their waiter, Tony, greeted them and James ordered without looking the menu. Tony delivered the starters quickly with a bottle of Chianti, two waters, bread and oil, and they shared a caprese salad. James made a perfect choice, as always, and Karen was really hungry after she took a quick peak at the menu. They sat comfortably on the patio content with each other. When Tony returned to take their entrée orders, Karen selected a creamy pasta and seafood combination; the carbohydrate load was beneficial after a day of hot sex. James ordered a filet mignon with a side of pasta and Karen hoped the entrée's arrived quickly before the wine went straight to her head. She didn't want to be drunk by dessert. James took her hand, "This is a day to remember. You were tremendous" and with that, they shared a passionate kiss at the table. James wasn't one for public displays of affection and Karen was pleasantly surprised that he boldly kissed her for all to see. She blushed as her cheeks flushed and she changed the subject quickly, "I'm starving and I think I ate the entire basket of bread before you even had a chance to touch it."

They sat on the deck and talked for more than 90 minutes over dinner. At Uncle Tony's they were never rushed with the check. Before dinner was over, James surprised Karen with an impromptu trip. They were off to Paris! He had an overseas meeting and promised dinner, shows, and shopping if she agreed to go with him. She never saw herself taking a "quick" trip to Paris but when you travel the way James did, anything was possible. The flight was long but with reclining sleeper seats on the plane, they should be able to arrive rested. They talked excitedly about their agenda while they finished the bottle of wine and then capped off the meal with Spanish coffees. They had no room for dessert and decided to walk around town to "people watch" before they returned home. James relaxed onto a bench where they sat quietly and watched the foot traffic window shop.

Danger lurked in the shadows next to Patti Cakes as Axel watched the same foot traffic. He never let the couple out of his sight and followed them as they traversed the docks back to the condo. Once they were inside the unit, Axel stepped into his rental boat already tied at the dock near their entrance. He sat and stalked them from the water. The couple was once again in Newport together; he pretended he had a rifle in his arms, pointed, and mouthed the expression "boom." He had one more day in town to finish the job.

CHAPTER THIRTY-THREE

It was still dark outside when Axel opened his eyes. The clock radio next to his twin bed glowed 4:50 am in red. Karen and James' schedule was routine and they usually left the condo between 8:00 and 9:00 am for coffee and/or breakfast. Axel was in the rental boat by 6:30 am as the rest of the town started their workdays. Since the couples' schedules rarely varied, Axel stationed himself in the rental boat to finish the contract once and for all. He kept busy with a fishing pole while he waited for them to step outside the condo. While he tinkered with a snagged reel, he saw them emerge a lot earlier than their usual start time. It was just before 7:00 am, and their driver was with them, another anomaly. Unfortunately, the driver carried suitcases which meant another trip. Axel had no idea where the couple might be off to now and no clue know how long they might be gone. He didn't want to do it but he called Jorge because he had no place to stay to ride out another trip. His rental was just about up with no luck finding alternate accommodations.

Axel despised the noise and congestion of Newport during tourist season anyway and Jorge suggested he return home for now. Jorge promised assistance while Axel regrouped locally for the next few days. Jorge had countless resources at his disposal, and it shouldn't take long for him to locate and determine James' whereabouts rather than Axel trying to do it locally. Once a new plan was in place Axel could complete the job. Jorge wasn't worried, and he assured Axel he wasn't upset with his efforts thus far.

By 2:00pm that same afternoon, Axel returned the rental boat in pristine condition. The owner was impressed, "I think the boat looks better than it did before you left. Thank you for taking such good care of it. Did you catch many fish while you were out?" Axel wasn't one for small talk. He half smiled and left without saying goodbye. He longed for the familiar sounds of home in the family garage working with his father, and his thoughts drifted as he made his way back to the airport for his 7:20 evening flight.

While Karen and James were off on a whirlwind trip to Paris, Miguel was somewhat of a recluse after Jill's death. He left his condo only once per day and he hadn't been back to his property in Brazil for months. His daily routine included one outing at precisely 3:30 PM where he proceeded to the mausoleum, where Jill's tomb was. His driver stopped the car within walking distance of the Rotunda and patiently waited in the parking lot while Miguel sat in front Jill's vault lamenting over what could have been. Miguel had a reputation as a lady's man and never met anyone marriage worthy until Jill. He respected, loved and cherished her. While he tried to get back to business, he wasn't ready to travel too far from her gravesite. The loss was just too great. He grieved in his own way and often punished himself for not doing more to protect her that fateful night.

Axel arrived back in Brazil on Friday, and Jorge visited the garage early Monday morning. Just as they did on the first visit, the two men used the dirty station office for a private conversation. Jorge had already located Karen and James. With his fortune, he had the means to buy information quickly. The couple was in Paris, and Miguel was still in Boca Raton. Jorge was too impatient to wait for Karen and James to return from France; therefore, he instructed Axel to kill Miguel now out of the original order that was in the contract. He presented a plane ticket that Axel placed in his shirt pocket, and the two men were in agreement. Mr. Vascone Sr. paid no attention to Jorge and as he worked under the hood of car with a transmission problem. Axel informed his father that he was leaving Tuesday morning, and he answered with a nod. There were no other questions asked and no further details provided.

Axel touched down in Orlando Tuesday night. He picked up a rental car and drove for about an hour, to the Embassy Suites in Boca Raton. Too tired to unpack, he collapsed on the bed fully clothed and fell into a deep sleep within minutes. He woke the next morning at 5:00 am, organized his clothes in the dresser drawers, showered, and made coffee from the machine in the hotel room. He spread the map of the area on the dinette table and realized he was very close to Miguel's already; the proximity left him time to make a second cup of coffee before he had to leave. He didn't buy any food ahead of time as he had done in Newport, so the coffee sufficed for now.

There were two equidistant routes from the hotel to the condo. It was a 5.6-mile drive if he took the main thoroughfare and he decided to head south on Route 1 since it was a busy road where he could blend into the traffic. He stopped for a quick breakfast and then waited in the shadows while he watched his next victim. Axel noted Miguel's daily routine while he surveyed the area for the perfect spot to kill him undetected. He sat in the car for six hours on the first day before Miguel finally emerged from the luxury condominium complex on Royal Palm Road. He noted the time, 3:30 pm. Miguel looked thinner than he did in the photograph Jorge gave him. He also noted that a driver took him everywhere so Miguel was never alone.

Through his reconnaissance efforts, Axel confirmed that Miguel left from the condo only once a day. It was the same routine; he hurriedly approached the car, was shown into the back seat, and the car pulled away. Axel followed behind them 2 or 3 car lengths away. Miguel's silver Mercedes pulled into the Boca Raton Mausoleum located on 4th Avenue after a five-minute drive. Axel pulled over to the side of a drive once inside because he could clearly see the car once they were inside the confines of the grounds. He stood in front of a random gravesite while he kept the Mercedes in view. The car pulled up to a round structure and Miguel went in alone. After 10 minutes, he reemerged and got into the backseat without waiting for the driver to open the door. Axel followed them out of the cemetery and back to the condo on East Royal Palm Rd. This time, Miguel waited for the driver to open the door, then retreated inside the condo. Axel waited curbside until 10:00 PM, but Miguel never came out again.

Axel stopped for food on the way back to the hotel, he was hungry since all he had was breakfast. After he ate, he packed a small "stake-out" satchel with fruits, nuts and water. He didn't watch TV once he was back in his room, instead he studied the map one more time and fell asleep by 11:30 pm. At 5:00 AM he woke and readied to plant himself in front of the condo for another full day of recon.

On the second day, it was more of the same. Miguel never left the condo until he appeared curbside at 3:30 PM. The driver showed him to the back seat, as customary, and Axel once again followed them to the cemetery. This time however, he followed Miguel inside the Rotunda. He stopped at a vault door, where once again, he made it appear he visited a deceased loved one. Miguel proceeded to Jill's vault, kissed his fingertips and touched the small door on the wall. He stood at the vault quietly with his hand on the steel door as he traced the inscription. He brought his hand to his lips one more time, touched the marker, and left. Axel walked over to the door and read the inscription. It was Jill Freeman's vault that Miguel visited every day. Axel studied the interior of the rotunda until he found an appropriate place to hide. Miguel would meet his fate soon.

Axel's return trip to Brazil was on Friday evening at 8:30 PM Now that he had a plan in place, he ran through the timeline quite a few times. Miguel was a creature of habit. At 3:30 PM every day, he was in the same place, and Axel allowed plenty of time in the schedule to kill him and get back to the airport in time for his return flight. As long as no one else was in the rotunda between 3:45 and 4:00 PM on Friday, that visit would be Miguel's last.

Miguel emerged from the condo at the regular time on Friday and proceeded to the cemetery right on schedule. Axel drove there ahead of them and parked behind the Rotunda. He entered the building from a rear door that was on the opposite side of the visitor parking lot. The back door was reserved for staff; therefore, he was hidden from Miguel's driver, or anyone else who may have visited that day.

When Miguel arrived, he proceeded to Jill's vault. As he stood in quiet reflection, something tightened around his neck and he couldn't breathe. He never even heard anyone come up behind him. His arms flailed in vain as he attempted to hit whoever was choking him, but the chord tightened around his neck, he couldn't free himself, and he gasped for air. Axel was so strong that he lifted Miguel slightly off the ground as he strangled him. Miguel never had a chance, and just before he lost consciousness, Axel whispered in his ear, "this is from your Uncle Jorge." Miguel's eyes widened with fear, and after three more excruciatingly painful minutes passed, there was nothing but darkness. His limp body quietly landed on the cold tile floor.

Axel pulled Miguel over near a bench, quickly scanned the room to be sure it was still empty, and removed Miguel's wallet, watch, and sunglasses to make it appear like a robbery. He left the mausoleum by the back door as quietly as he entered, found his car where he had left it in the back lot, and drove out of the cemetery on schedule. Miguel's driver patiently waited in front of the rotunda, and Axel drove by him without eye contact from either driver.

On the way to the airport, Axel tossed Miguel's personal items out the window every few miles along the highway. The items may or may not ever be found, and even if they were discovered, they were a long way away from Boca Raton. Axel tried on Miguel's sunglasses and liked the way they blocked the sun, but he couldn't keep them. After another mile, he tossed them out the passenger side window while he was in the far right-hand lane.

After 20 minutes, Miguel's driver became concerned about his boss because he deviated from the normal routine, and quietly entered the Rotunda to check on him. He found Miguel's lifeless body perched against the bench and called 911. The ambulance arrived and EMT's raced into the rotunda. After a quick assessment, they slowly wheeled Miguel out of the building and whisked him away to the hospital. It was obvious to the medics, and the sedan driver, that Miguel was dead. The ER physician contacted the local police and reported Miguel dead upon arrival from an apparent strangulation. It didn't take long before Miguel's death was ruled a homicide.

CHAPTER THIRTY-FOUR

When their two-week vacation came to an end, Karen was eager to get back to work. The "quick trip" to Paris lasted a lot longer than planned. They had such a grand time, that they extended the trip and turned it into a real vacation. The extension meant Karen needed a few new outfits and James had a chance to spoil her. She did her best not to gasp at the prices in the designer boutiques as James proudly produced his credit card for every purchase. She loved being pampered and the trip did a world of good for their relationship.

They casually strolled the streets of Paris arm in arm, while they cleared the air of old grievances. James promised to trust her judgment going forward and vowed to stay off her back while she freelanced for the FBI. He also professed that he had never met anyone like her and Karen was flattered by the praise. Unlike most of the people in James' sphere, Karen wasn't motivated by money and during one of their lengthy talks he admitted that he tried to buy her out of working falsely thinking that if he threw enough money at her, she might have acquiesced and quit her job, but he knew better now, and appreciated her even more for it. They had a new level of understanding and strengthened their relationship which was why they extended their trip for an extra week. Paris is a beautiful city. They went to the Opera, saw two plays, and enjoyed Parisian pastries as they window shopped. On James' free mornings, that sat outside at a café near the hotel. James took a few business calls over breakfast but was always careful not to overdo it, and gave Karen his full attention.

They dined at Le George at the Four Season's on their last night. They were a handsome couple with James in a tuxedo, Karen in her long black dress adorned with a new diamond necklace and matching bracelet. All told, Karen wore at least 24 carats of diamonds that night, and they looked like royalty. The meal was exquisite, and James' command of the French language was impressive. Karen wasn't entirely sure what he ordered, but he sounded so sexy as he spoke, she could have had pizza and been happy. They dined at a late seating and returned to their room around midnight. Once they were alone, Karen dropped her dress to the floor and James admired her jewelry.

The couple returned to Providence before noon the next day, and Karen looked forward to coffee with the girls after her two-week adventure. They had agreed to meet at 9:00 AM at the bakery. Karen left early to immerse herself in the familiar sights and scents of the waterfront. It was only a five-minute walk but she took the long route to window shop on the way. She bumped into Gloria on the way, and they hugged when they saw each other. "It's been ages, how was Paris?"

"It was just what we needed. I had a really nice time, but I better not tell you too much now or Patti will be jealous!" The friends chatted as they walked the last few hundred feet to Patti Cakes.

Patti was already outside at their designated table and her voice bellowed down the street as Gloria and Karen neared, "now there's a sight for sore eyes, get your asses over here and let's have a group hug!" Patti was loud but a joy to be around. "How was Paris?"
"Better than I could have imagined. When James worked, I went shopping and sat in outdoor cafes missing you ladies."
"I hope their pastry wasn't better than mine."
"No way Patti, you are the best and no one in Paris can hold a candle to you!" The trio was happy to be reunited and Karen had lots to share.

Gloria appeared quieter than usual. During the visit she touched Karen's hand, "I'm so sorry about your friend, I feel responsible."
"Oh Gloria, there wasn't anything you or I could have done differently. Please don't blame yourself. Have the police made any progress in the investigation while I've been away?" Gloria didn't know much more but relayed the tiny bits of information she had. To Karen, it looked like the investigation was exactly where it was before she left on her trip. The police believed Jill was shot by accident while they aimed for Devon Smith. The shooter was likely in a boat in the harbor, or on foot near the harbor but they had no clue as to the identity or motive of the assailant. Gloria didn't know how they determined the shooter was in the harbor

but Karen was familiar with the ammunition used and it sounded like a logical conclusion.

When the trio finally parted ways after two espressos and banana muffins, Karen and Gloria left together. Gloria extended a lunch invitation; she wanted to hear more about Paris since she had never been there. Karen happily accepted the invite since James was spending the day busy in his office and, if she wasn't home, he could concentrate without being distracted. Gloria had a treat in store this time, Heavy D's son Markis was at the house and Karen could finally meet him.

The ladies dined on the upper-level deck with the wrap around porch which provided a beautiful view of the harbor. Mid-way through the meal, Gloria excused herself and when she returned, Markis was with her. It was a bit shocking to see how much he looked like his father. People often used the adage 'chip off the old block,' and it was uncanny, Markis looked like a younger version of his father. Heavy D fondly referred to Markis as "Little D", meaning little Devon. Markis longed to be just like his Dad and he was proud of the nickname. Karen only imagined what boarding school was like for him. He was so young to be schooled that far away from home and, since his mother died many years ago, he was probably lonely so far away. If it wasn't for Gloria, Markis wouldn't have had much attention at all since Heavy D wasn't around much.

Gloria doted on him as if he was her son. Her hand was always on him somewhere, whether she touched his shoulder or stroked his hair when he was within reach. She clearly loved him and he glanced at her with the same affection. Markis was a very polite, well-spoken young man. Gloria walked him back to his room where he restarted his video game.

She returned fairly quickly, "I'm glad you had the chance to meet him, he is a delightful boy and very special to me."

"It is obvious how much you love him and he's lucky to have you."

Gloria had a look of concern and Karen asked what was on her mind, "you look worried about something, is everything alright"?

"Devon hasn't been the same since the shooting. I know it must be shocking to think someone wants to kill you, but he is anxious all the time and he won't let me or Markis out of his sight. That's the reason I am living here now and not on the boat."

"You decided to move in?"

"It wasn't my choice. When I went to the boat after work one day, my clothes were gone, and I thought I was robbed. I called Devon and he said he moved my things to the house. He wants me to stay here until the shooter is caught. I couldn't believe he violated my space like that without asking. I feel a bit trapped and not quite sure what to do about it. You simply don't say no to Devon."

"Oh Gloria, I'm sorry. I hate to hear you and Devon are struggling. Truth be told, I flew back from Florida by myself after Jill's funeral while James stayed back at the beach house. We had an argument; he said he wasn't coming back with me and expected me to stay there with him. I thought it was over and caught the next flight back here without him. After a miserable day of not talking, we connected later that night. When we took the trip to Paris, we talked more. I'm telling you all of this because I understand how you feel. Devon should have talked to you before moving you into his house. That was a violation of your space and your trust. Talk to him and work it out. The longer you hold it in the more resentment you'll have, and if you wait too long it might be too late."

"I'm sorry you and James had a fight but I'm glad you worked it out and you're right, I will talk to him when he's back at the house tonight. He spends most of time at the office on the other property nowadays. He won't meet anyone here, because we're here, and we aren't allowed there. He won't jeopardize our safety."

The two women talked like old friends for another hour. Karen will miss Gloria when the case was over, and while it was a long shot, she hoped Gloria would stay in Markis' life once Heavy D was incarcerated. Gloria briefly mentioned Miguel during their visit and Karen had a twinge of guilt because she hadn't spoken to him in weeks. She made a mental note to reach out to him when she got back home. Around 2:30 pm, Karen took in one last deep breath of fresh salty air and the women ended their lunch engagement.

CHAPTER THIRTY-FIVE

James was on a conference call when Karen returned and, after a quickly mouthed hello, she went to her office and phoned Mark. Unfortunately, the FBI hadn't turned up any new information on the shooter even though they knew the names of many of Heavy D's associates. The taskforce tracked down Heavy D's known enemies, all of whom were accounted for, and none were in the local area the night of the shooting. The taskforce yielded some new information, however; one of Heavy Ds associates was confirmed on multiple trips to Cartagena, Columbia. That was the first clue that linked Heavy D to the drug business overseas. Rebecca, the missing college student, was also last tracked traveling there. The investigation moved forward piece by piece as Mark relayed all the specifics during the call while Karen listened intently.

Even after all the information she had, she was surprised that Heavy D was at the helm of a large drug cartel. He alone was responsible for the movement of approximately 200 kilos of cocaine a year worth about $18M-$20M a year. Add to that his legitimate businesses which brought in another $8-$10million and it was easy to see why Devon Smith was a very wealthy man. Karen never thought he had the ingenuity to develop such a vast and sophisticated network, but the numbers didn't lie.

Most of the Heavy D's product was smuggled into the country by boat through a port in Miami then driven to a small-town in South Carolina. There were two auto body shops in Dunean that prepped vehicles to transport drugs largely undetected. The product was dropped at a warehouse, and workers outfitted transport vehicles with special compartments to house the drugs. The product was then driven to points north to distribution hubs in New York City and Providence, Rhode Island. Heavy D had a partner in NYC who he trusted implicitly. They had been friends since childhood, belonged to the same street gang, and were brothers, if not by blood.

The drug cartel's network was vast. The route started in Columbia, came through Panama, then on to Miami. Occasionally, if passage was too risky the load was driven from Columbia through the Darien Gap into Mexico, then shipped from there to Miami. The latter was a deadly trek and the men responsible for those shipments were ruthless killers. The FBI had an undercover agent in one of the body shops in South Carolina, but Karen was the only person with direct access to the big man himself, and Mark stressed the importance of her continued involvement. "Karen, we haven't been this close in years, and I can feel our break coming soon. Do what you can to learn about his travel schedule. We want to get him on camera making a deal. This guy is careful and we don't have what we need yet." After surveilling Heavy D's alternate office, Mark was convinced the property was used for more than boarding horses, and Karen had to get inside that facility for a closer look.

Before their call ended, Karen asked about Rebecca Jones. Mark's response wasn't encouraging. "We have no new information on her, but we're not giving up, I promise."

The call ended and Karen reran the lunch conversation she had with Gloria. She spent most of their time together listening while Gloria prattled on about Devon's humanitarian efforts. She cringed at the thought of Devon referred to as a humanitarian. The more Karen learned about the desperate young students Heavy D preyed upon, the angrier she got. One of Heavy D's lieutenants coerced innocent college students to become drug smugglers, "mules" as Heavy D aptly put it, and she wanted to arrest him herself! Thanks to Mark, she learned a lot more about the many layers of his organization and it was clear, he was loathsome. Karen was more determined than ever to see Heavy D held accountable for his crimes. She recalled Gloria mentioned the use of the stables for meetings now that Markis was home, Heavy D never wanted his son exposed to the business, and Keren needed a plausible excuse to get on to the property with or without Gloria.

As their friendship deepened, Karen understood why Gloria was kept at arms' length in her relationship with Heavy D. He had a lot to hide from everyone and, while he trusted Gloria, he kept her in the dark about most of his business dealings. Karen often wondered how Gloria could be that gullible to trust him with blind faith when she was obviously a smart and savvy woman in her own right. Karen learned a lot about Heavy D through their casual conversations and fed that information back to the FBI investigators.

CHAPTER THIRTY-SIX

A trusted confidante of Heavy D, the "handler," managed the student drug transport program. This wasn't a main source of income, but it was another means to keep the flow of drugs consistent. The handler's sole job was to recruit college students to transport cocaine into the U.S. Heavy D had no direct involvement in the program, in fact, he never gave it much thought, and was only notified when a drug run went awry. Thankfully for those involved, it was rare that a carrier went rogue. The pool of candidates came from two local colleges, the handler receiving their names and contact information from the financial aid office workers on the cartel payroll. It was a simple cash transaction. The list of students didn't cost much and there was a never-ending supply to pick from.

The potential smugglers/students were targeted based on their financial needs and their naiveté. The handler usually met the student at a nearby coffee shop and, once he got to know them, he presented an opportunity to earn cash for their tuition. He posed it as an "easy assignment" and made the offer too good to pass up. The handler, whose given name was Winslow, was a childhood friend of Heavy D's, and kept in regular contact with two administrators at Johnston and Whales University and the University of Rhode Island. The administrators received $1,000 each time Winslow requested a new target list. Winslow never disclosed his intentions, but the administrators appreciated the additional cash and never asked questions.

When Winslow found the right student desperate enough to take the bait, he offered $5,000 and a free trip to an exotic destination during spring break. He asked them to retrieve a package and assured them there was very little risk in the assignment. He casually introduced himself as John Smith and joked with the student that even though his name sounded fake, he really was named John Smith. He slyly said he wasn't sure what his parents were thinking when they came up with that name. The uneasy student usually laughed along with Winslow, and the rapport slowly began. He went on to explain there was even more money for additional trips once the student committed to the plan. He closed the conversation and confirmed that others took the same trip many times, returned safely, and made a lot of money. Winslow was a savvy negotiator and reminded the student about their mountain of tuition debts throughout the conversation. He sounded sincere when he explained that he was there only to help.

The unsuspecting student had no idea what kind of package they had to retrieve but probably suspected it was something illegal. Winslow set the student up to smuggle 2-3 kilos of cocaine back to the US to earn the payout. Those selected were carefully vetted and no one signed on until multiple discussions had taken place. Winslow had to be sure. The student got to know "John Smith" and thought of him as an older friend. If the student accepted the job, it was because they needed the money bad enough that they ignored the risks. The students ranged in age between 18-20 years old. At that age, they considered themselves invincible which made them great carrier candidates. However, before the trip, it was very clear – they can't talk to anyone about their business arrangement, or the deal was off. There was an unspoken veil of threat woven throughout the conversation. The mule, as Winslow called them, had their bags outfitted to carry cocaine once only they were in too deep to back out. The program hardly seemed worth the time, effort, and risk but the organization needed their help periodically and Heavy D claimed it was his way to help less fortunate pay for college. He considered the risk-reward balance evenly split. The students earned enough money to cover the costs of a semester, and Heavy D got drugs into the country without any direct involvement; everyone won.

When a student finally landed in sunny Columbia, usually after being routed there through Mexico, they were picked up at the airport and taken to a modest home by a local partner. The student had a day or two of free time to lounge by the pool while they rehearsed the very specific travel instructions that must be followed to return to the US safely. They were well cared for but never allowed to leave the house while they waited to return home. It was a short vacation.

Travel plans were very specific, and it was the mule's job to memorize the itinerary. The cartel had paid agents at the airport to ease passage through customs and mules travel was dependent on the agents' schedules. Mules studied their photographs and did their homework relaxing by the pool. It was imperative the mules remembered those faces before they got to the airport since their lives depended on it.

Once at the airport, the mule found the right agent and sailed through security without incident. However, when a mule got shifted to the wrong line, it was devastating. Their bag was flagged after it passed through the x-ray machine, and they were on their own to save themselves. It was very clear that they didn't want to do that! The thought of never making it out of Cartagena, Columbia was so terrifying that the mules did their homework. John Smith, of course, was untraceable.

Once the mule made it through security at the airport in Columbia, their return trip to the U.S. came through one of two entry points, either a trek through Mexico City - Houston - Providence, or through Miami back to Providence. Their toughest hurdle was getting through US customs. Heavy D had a TSA employee on the payroll at the Houston airport and three paid agents at the Miami airport. As long as the students travelled when they were supposed to travel, and selected the correct security line, they got through customs without a problem.

From the Houston or Miami airport, the mules flew back to Providence where Winslow met them in the short-term parking lot right outside the terminal. It was the same process every time. Winslow tossed the mules duffle bag in the trunk, or the back of the truck, and the student was driven back to college $5K richer. The program usually ran smoothly.

However, there were times when a student had ideas of grandeur. In one case, a mule tried to sell the haul on their own to the highest bidder. They found a buyer outside the hotel who offered them $20K. That mule was dealt with swiftly because Winslow had eyes everywhere. He ran the program with an iron fist, and disloyalty to the organization was a death sentence. All students were closely monitored, and it was rare anyone tried to double cross Winslow but when it happened, the student was killed and discarded in a foreign country never to be seen again.

CHAPTER THIRTY-SEVEN

The TSA kept a close eye on screeners in the Houston and Miami airports after a tip from the FBI. Multiple agencies worked in tandem on the case against Devon Smith, and they were on heightened alert. Agency leaders were notified as new information became available as the case again Heavy D solidified. Mark spoke directly with the TSA chiefs in both airports, and they agreed to contact him if any traveler arrived with a kilo or more of drugs on their person.

Jason Andrews, a student from Providence College, the latest mule, was unexpectedly caught coming through customs in Miami. He had three kilos of cocaine in his duffle bag and ended up in the wrong line with the wrong agent. This time, Winslow wasn't alerted to his arrest because of schedule changes. Jason was swiftly and uneventfully removed from the screening area. The drugs were discovered concealed in the lining of his bag despite being covered with a special film that blocked the odor and image of the cocaine. The TSA agent Jason was supposed to use was called away from his post at the last minute, and the replacement agent was not on the cartel payroll. Jason panicked and tried to change lines, and the disruption raised suspicion. He was directed to a different conveyor where it was X-rayed by another machine. Once he was flagged for an additional search, he knew it was trouble. He was politely escorted to a holding room behind the security screening area. Sweat began under his clothes as he walked with the agent. He tried to stop his hands from shaking but had no idea what to do and absolutely no one to call. He was uncertain of his fate but knew not to say a word to anyone.

The TSA Chief called Mark at headquarters in Boston and informed him of Jason's arrest. He also noted the size of the seizure. The Chief was surprised by Mark's response. He asked that Jason be released on to the flight and assured the Chief he would be arrested in Providence the minute he exited the aircraft. He also asked that Jason's bag be placed with the other luggage near the front of the cargo hold guaranteeing the bag will be retrieved by an FBI agent when they landed. Reluctantly, the Chief agreed.

The TSA Chief returned to the holding cell and to Jason's shock, he was free to go. His bag was checked through to his final destination as a courtesy. Jason was dumfounded he wasn't arrested, and while he remained uneasy, he assumed Winslow had a hand in his release. The Chief didn't want Jason to call anyone, so he informed him that he was the victim of a mistaken identity. Even more surprising, the Chief apologized for holding him! He claimed there was another Jason Andrews on the TSA no-fly list because of suspected terrorist activities, and they got the two men confused. The Chief seemed contrite while Jason remained stoically seated in the holding room. He couldn't believe his luck to have gotten out of this jam and breathed a huge sigh of relief. He was ever so gracious to the agent who escorted him back to the gate and was walking calmly as he boarded the plane home free.

***

Back in Boston, the taskforce assigned agents on the ground at TF Green airport. The small tactical team had to retrieve the black duffle bag as soon as the plane landed, then whisk the bag to the TSA office where it will be outfitted with a GPS device. The bag will be tossed back into the pile of checked luggage and arrive on the carousel at baggage claim for Jason to retrieve. Mark spoke to the local agent who was 30 minutes outside the airport. Agent Stripley was charged with the arrangements on the ground, and they had a few hours to get their plans in place before the plane arrived. He understood Mark's intensity while they went over the details during the call. They were close to an arrest and Agent Stripley was ready to go. The team must secure the bag of drugs without anyone noticing, then Agent Stripley had to get Jason Andrews to talk within the first 20 minutes after landing. They needed to flip Jason to their side before he reconnected with Winslow.

Mark and the agent outlined the terms of Jason's deal over the phone during the ride to the airport. The deal was pretty simple, if Jason agreed to cooperate, he won't be charged with trafficking. If he refuses to talk, he's arrested on the spot, and will spend much of his life in prison. The deal was a no-brainer. The FBI was poised and ready at the airport, and Mark was as close as he had been to finally making an arrest. Jason was a solid link in the evidence chain, and everything depended on Agent Stripley's next conversation. It was a tense afternoon.

Just before the plane touched down in Providence, a flight attendant asked Jason to move up to 1st class due to a family emergency. She was just notified from the pilot. He reluctantly moved to the new seat as requested, but the so-called "emergency," wasn't good news. He had no family so the seat change meant the police were likely waiting for him when the door opens, and it was doubtful John Smith was in the parking lot waiting for him. He stayed as calm as he could, but it was difficult under the circumstances. When the door of the plane unlocked, Agent Stripley was waiting for Jason. He wasn't handcuffed but ordered to follow him up the ramp and was, once again, escorted to an airport holding cell.

Once Jason was seated, Agent Stripley laid out the charges. They discovered 3 kilos of cocaine in his bag in Miami and he was in a lot of trouble. Jason had a moment to process the seriousness of the situation before Stripley put the deal on the table. Jason was promised immunity if he provided the names of every person he was in contact with and every stop he made while he traveled to and from Cartagena. If the information led to an arrest, the charges against him would be dropped. Jason was apprehensive because he didn't know the names, but new the faces from the pictures he memorized. He was confident, he could identify them in a photo lineup. Jason pleaded for the chance to help himself. Stripley checked his watch. Jason had been in the holding cell for 15 minutes and had to exit the terminal soon or the handler would know something happened and leave without him. If that happens, the entire ground effort would be a bust.

Jason Andrews, the frightened freshman from Providence College, confessed that never met Devon Smith nor did he ever hear his name. Agent Stripley hammered him specifically for information about Devon Smith aka Heavy D. Jason had no idea who was in charge of the operation besides his handler, John Smith. The only other person Jason ever heard mentioned was the generic term of the "boss", but the boss was never given a name. Jason spoke with one person and one person only, John Smith, the same person who was picking him up at the airport and dropping him back at school. Jason nervously explained the photo array he was required to memorize. For now, they had to let him go but assured him they would be waiting for him. It was a final warning so Jason wouldn't run.

Agent Stripley tossed the duffle bag back to Jason. He was released from custody a second time, and quickly raced to the exit doors to meet the handler in the short-term parking lot according to plan. John Smith sat in the truck unbothered as Jason approached. He got out, tossed duffle bag into the trunk, returned to the front seat, and drove Jason back to college blissfully unaware of the tracking device the FBI had in the strap of Jason's bag.

John Smith pulled up in front of the dorm, handed Jason payment for the transport, and drove off with the drugs. When Jason entered the dorm, an agent was there waiting and escorted him out the back entrance. Jason Andrews knew he was in trouble and as the two men walked to the agents' car, Jason promised to fully cooperate with the FBI investigation.

The taskforce had a watchful eye on the entire route of the duffle bag on a screen in their field office. Mark had a dry grin as they followed the car directly to Heavy D's stables. He clapped both hands hard since he had the link he'd been waiting for. Now that the drugs were on site, Karen had a crucial role in the final phase of the investigation. Three kilos of cocaine were important, but it wasn't enough to put Heavy D away for life. Mark was a patient man; he was nearing an arrest and he owed Karen an update.

Heavy D's organization was a complicated web. Karen often wondered if Heavy D's arrest would really make a dent in the vast number of drugs brought into the US every year. However, because of her own personal vendetta, she wasn't giving up because she wanted him behind bars. She sat in her office a while longer while she reviewed the case file the agents amassed on Heavy D. She couldn't help but wonder, "was Gloria really that naïve, or had she known all along what her boyfriend was up to?" It was hard to believe Devon Smith could manage a multi-million drug ring right under her nose and she never saw or heard a thing. Gloria seemed smarter than that.

CHAPTER THIRTY-EIGHT

It took Karen at least another hour to get caught up on her mail when it dawned on her she never checked in on Miguel. On her first try, the call went directly to voice mail and she left a message. Her second call a few hours later also went straight to voice mail. He was struggling and she wondered how he was coping since Jill's passing. It was somewhat of a comfort that Miguel and Jill found each other in the first place even though their relationship was cut tragically short. In reality, Karen didn't really know that much about Miguel, but considered him a friend, and would check in on him again tomorrow. He must be busy.

James finally emerged from his office and, when they met in the kitchen, Karen asked, "I tried to get ahold of Miguel this evening and my calls went right to voice mail. Have you spoken to him recently by chance?"

"I haven't talked to him; he is more your friend than mine. When was the last time you talked to him?"

"It was before Paris I think."

"I'm sure he is just busy. Let's go eat, I'm starving."

With that, James and Karen walked into town for dinner. They were busy most of the day and, even though they were in the same house, they hadn't spoken to each since breakfast, and she had a lot to tell him.

On their walk home after dinner, James sensed Karen unease over Miguel's silence. He called Kevin for a favor. Kevin was at the beach house and James asked him to take a swing by Miguel's condo just to make sure he was okay. Kevin didn't join the couple when they returned to Newport after their disagreement, he stayed behind at the beach house, and it was handy having him in Florida now to make a quick trip over to Miguel's. They enjoyed their peaceful walk back the condo and it was almost 11:00 pm by the time they got ready for bed. Karen was in the bathroom undressing when she heard James' phone ring. She poked her head out of the bathroom while she brushed her teeth and James was on the phone looking concerned during the call. His face said it all, something was wrong.

He motioned her to sit down on the bed next to him as the call continued. When he hung up, he delivered the awful news. "You aren't going to believe this - Miguel is dead." Karen was shocked and found it hard to fathom that another one of her friends was dead. James continued, "Kevin talked to a bodyguard at Miguel's this evening, and he told him what he knew. Miguel's driver took him to the cemetery every day to visit Jill's gravesite. Miguel was usually inside for 10 minutes while the driver waited in the car for him. When Miguel's visit ran longer than usual, the driver went inside to check on him and found Miguel on the floor unresponsive."

Miguel was robbed and it appeared there was a struggle between him and the attacker. Karen leapt up from the bed, "I want to go to Florida immediately." James wasn't surprised by her reaction but hoped she changed her mind by morning once the news settled.

Karen was unstoppable when she made a decision. If she was going to Florida, James was going with her. Karen had a strong sense of responsibility to Jill; therefore, she was intent on a trip to Florida. The two girlfriends promised each other to watch out for their men, and Karen wanted to uphold that promise by helping local police however she could while they investigated Miguel's murder. She owed it to Jill.

They crawled under the covers and Karen's thoughts swirled round and round over the news of Miguel's sudden death. She also couldn't shake the feeling that someone was after all four of them. Miguel's and Jill's deaths couldn't just be awful coincidences. Once she dug into the robbery and Miguel's murder, she hoped to either prove a connection or dispel her unease. She sensed dread. Could someone really be after the four of them? Her mind wandered back to the murders in Brazil. She retraced her steps of that fateful day when the murderers were blown to bits on their yacht. She had a few burning questions. Did someone survive that explosion? Did someone know what they did? Dark thoughts weighed her down and she didn't sleep despite being exhausted.

By now, James was breathing heavily enough that he was sound asleep. Karen was so restless she contemplated getting out of bed but stayed put and focused on her breathing - in through her nose and out through her mouth – as she tried to relax. She nestled in closer to James who instinctively put his arm around her. At that moment, she was calm. Before nodding off, she made a mental list of the information for the Florida police. First, they needed to know about Jill's connection to Miguel, where she worked, how they met, and a timeline of events that led to Jill's death in Newport. As the Florida police worked the investigation on Miguel, the information Karen had should show a connection between the two murders. Karen was there to help, that much she can do for her friend, and she finally drifted off to sleep confident the trip to Florida was the right thing to do.

Over breakfast, James phoned his assistant, and she booked the jet. Karen promised James repeatedly she only planned to talk to the police, not to try to solve the case for them. She had no spare time to simultaneously investigate Miguel's murder and work on Heavy D's case with the FBI, therefore, she counted on the local detectives to do a thorough investigation. If no connection was found between her friends' murders, she would rest easier. The potential peace of mind made the trip that much more worthwhile.

CHAPTER THIRTY-NINE

Karen and James arrived in Florida on time and Kevin was waiting for them. He was happy to see them together though he never said it aloud. The last time all three of them were in the same place was at the beach house, where they had a huge disagreement, and it wasn't a pleasant experience. That argument seemed so long ago now.

Before they left for Paris, James had Kevin return to Florida since they could manage on their own in Newport. Kevin had no time for a social life as James' personal assistant, and Karen never understood how anyone could do that job. Kevin lived in James' house and while he had his own quarters with a separate entrance, he was always on call wherever and whenever James needed him. Karen empathized and James reminded her that Kevin was paid handsomely, and he was good at his job. Not everyone was cut out to be a personal assistant and James was lucky to have a loyal, trusted employee. Kevin escorted Karen into the back seat and didn't hide his broad smile when she gave him a quick hug before she got in.

Once they were back at the beach house, Karen settled into her office and got right to work. She didn't have that much information to go on so her first call was to Anthony, an old tech friend from the Bureau. Anthony worked in cyberterrorism and was always busy, but never too busy for a call from Karen. They had been classmates at the FBI academy. Karen thought Anthony would have made a great field agent, but he was more interested in chasing criminals behind the scenes on a computer, than in the field on foot. He was a genius on the computer, and Karen never asked for information he or she shouldn't see. Of course, it was also nice for the two friends to connect and catch up.

After a minute or two of small talk, Anthony asked what she needed. She appreciated his no-nonsense style and asked him to review the police reports for Miguel's death, then compare them to the police reports filed in Jill's death to see if there were any similarities. That was the first request. The second request was based off a hunch. She wanted all persons traveling from Brazil to Providence and Brazil to Orlando during the weeks of their deaths. After a few questions, Anthony readily agreed, Karen thanked him and hung up. He had access to the information easily enough and, because he was an FBI analyst, he had a keen eye to discover links in cases that might not look so obvious to a police detective. He also had unlimited access to places on the web a local detective didn't have. When the call ended, she was confident the project was in the right hands as she readied to visit to the cemetery to pay her respects to Jill while she reviewed the crime scene increasingly aware that if her hunch was correct, it meant she and James were in real danger.

Karen swung by Miguel's condo before going to the cemetery and found one of his bodyguards in the lobby. He was the only employee on site and awaiting the arrival of Miguel's father Felix from Brazil. She remembered spending the day with Felix when they visited Miguel's ranch in Bahia Brazil, and she hoped to see him to offer sympathy when he arrived to accompany Miguel's remains back to Brazil for burial in their family plot. The employee in the lobby, Diego, was the last person to see Miguel alive. The police questioned him a number of times, but he didn't have much to tell. Diego's English wasn't very good, and Karen's Portuguese was even worse so it was difficult for them to communicate effectively, but she tried anyway. From what she gathered, Miguel didn't have any enemies who would want to hurt him. She gave Diego her number and asked that he give it to Felix.

After a short drive, she arrived at the cemetery thankful for the bright sunny day. The location was a quiet, peaceful, resting place that occupied a massive plot of land. The last time she was there, for Jill's service, she hardly remembered looking at anything except for the ground because it was such a dreadfully sad time. She parked in the lot outside the Rotunda, where the deceased vaults were kept, and took in a deep breath before she entered the building. As she approached Jill's marker, a wave of sadness washed over her. It's sad that she can't talk to her friend. While standing quietly for a moment, she asked Jill for help anyway. Maybe she heard her, and maybe she didn't, but it felt like the right thing to do as she searched for clues about Miguel's killer.

The Rotunda was a sizeable building with polished marble floors that looked like they were wet from the shine. The center of the room was well appointed with couches, candles and flowers. It was the perfect place for reflection with kneelers and candles along the walls in front of the deceased's remains. Karen remembered exactly where Jill's space was and reread the inscription on the door, "Life's journey has been all the better for you being in it." She traced the letters with her fingers and reminisced about her friend for another moment.

Karen scanned the Rotunda for security monitors but didn't find any inside the pristine space. She was alone in the building, and it was eerily quiet except for the faint sound of the AC unit that consistently blew cool air. She noted three exit doors, two led to the parking area, and the third led to the cemetery grounds. If Miguel's killer went out the third door, his driver wouldn't have seen him enter or leave the facility. It was a perfect place to commit a crime since there wasn't any security, and little to no foot traffic. Visitors were usually grief stricken and less likely to pay attention to anyone or anything around them.

Being thorough, she walked through the cemetery instead of relying on the details from the police report. Once back at the house, she found the phone number of the detective handling Miguel's case. She called him but he didn't appreciate her input on the case, nor was he impressed by her consulting position with the FBI. He scoffed at the suggestion that Jill's murder in Newport was connected with Miguel's murder in Boca Raton. The detective was quick to point out that he already knew about Jill Freeman's death and the only connection was that the two murders were unfortunate coincidences. He claimed he spoke to the Detective in Newport but can't recall his name. He clearly lied because Chuck Workman was the investigator in Newport, and his name was unique enough that the Florida detective would have remembered it. It wasn't worth her time to challenge his credibility, however. She turned over all the information she had, and the detective ended the call in a huff. He was clearly bothered that he offered to help.

Anthony called the next morning and somehow Karen missed the call. He left a message of sympathy for her loss, and had information, if she could call him back. She closed the door to her office for privacy and returned Anthony's call. He was a wealth of information, and she could hardly write it all down fast enough to keep up. Anthony methodically covered the complicated steps he took to track down the information. There were approximately 2000 people who flew from Brazil to Orlando during the week Miguel was killed but the list got much smaller when he considered only travelers who also flew to Providence the same week Jill was killed and ruled out families traveling with children.

When he dug deeper into the backgrounds of the remaining list of people he found an interesting hit. That traveler was Anthony's person of interest, a former GRUMEC with 8 years of service in the military. The Brazilian military rank of GRUMEC is much like a Navy SEAL, specially trained in an elite sector of the military who performed tasks such as reconnaissance, sabotage and elimination of targets of strategic value. The traveler was Axel Vascone, who left the military with an honorable discharge after 8 years of service. He currently worked as a mechanic at his father's garage in a poor section of downtown Salvador in the state of Bahia, Brazil. He had no prior record, warrants, or arrests. Anthony also had three other potential suspects, but they appeared to be legitimate business travelers since their travel didn't originate from Brazil; they only traveled through Brazil with multiple other stops along the way.

When Karen heard where Axel was from, she knew Anthony had found the right guy. He flew on one-way tickets to and from Providence pain in cash and it was logical that he knew Miguel's extended family since, they too lived Bahia. Her gut told her he was after her, but she didn't have enough information yet. She took copious notes and didn't say a word during the one-sided conversation with Anthony. He sent a photo of Axel to her phone; she didn't recognize him. His eyes looked dark yet piercing with a blank stare; something wasn't right about their suspect.

Axel flew from Orlando to Brazil the same day Miguel was murdered. Could Axel have killed Miguel in Boca Raton that afternoon and made an 8:00 pm flight in Orlando? She hoped the coroner could narrow down Miguel's time of death to answer that question. If it lined up, it could very well be possible Axel killed Miguel and hopped on a plane back to Brazil a few hours afterward. Axel's travel schedule was not a mere coincidence.

James quietly knocked on her office door, and opened it, just enough to poke his head in to check on her. She signaled "one minute" with her finger, and he backed out and waited for her in the kitchen. She thanked Anthony for his quick work and ended the call. Her instincts suggested that someone was after them. She opted not to tell James yet for fear he would try to put her into a protective bubble. Knowing that Axel returned to Brazil, they were safe for the time being, but she was going stick to James like glue over the coming weeks. A few questions begged to be answered....who the hell was Axel Vascone and why did he want to kill them?

James and Karen went for a nice long walk on the beach. She was eager to get her feet in the sand and feel the warmth of the sun on her face. An hour-long walk cleared her head and she put police work aside while she exercised with James. As they strolled along the shoreline, they agreed on their return date to Newport. Karen stayed focused and present in the conversation; however, now that she had a picture of the man who murdered her friends, that image was burned into her brain. She had to remain hyper vigilant to project James. Unfortunately, it wasn't hard to see that Karen was distracted. James assumed she missed her friends, or at least he hoped that's all it was. As they continued walking and talking, Karen participated in the conversation despite being unnerved because they were completely unprotected in the wide-open space on the beach. They were safer in Newport condo with multiple security gates, water, and a sophisticated alarm system. Now that they made plans to return, the thought eased her mind a bit.

CHAPTER FORTY

The couple was once again back in Newport after a 2-day stay in Florida. Karen never did catch up with Felix while they were there, but she left him a note and promised to attend Miguel's funeral once planned. For now, she resolved to focus on the investigation into Heavy D and vowed to find Axel Vascone. She reached out to Mark the first chance she got now that they were local.

The FBI and their counterparts in the DEA had a joint plan to dismantle Heavy D's organization. The plan was to intercept boats carrying drugs into Florida, and they had agents in place ready to go. Simultaneously they would raid four body shops in South Carolina looking for those responsible for outfitting special car compartments to transport cocaine to points north. The manpower assigned to this case was impressive and she hoped to see Heavy D in prison for a very long time once they started arresting people. The taskforce agents needed Heavy D caught in the act, or even better, record him discussing drug related business on tape. After a lengthy investigation, they didn't have enough evidence against him just yet but they were close and their plan was ready. Once they had a warrant to search his domicile and office building, they hoped to unearth enough evidence to arrest him.

Mark asked Karen to get inside the riding stables in Portsmouth, RI as soon as possible. Heavy D held meetings there and the FBI didn't have a camera or listening device inside the building. Almost daily, Heavy D's security team swept his office for monitoring devices, and the alarm system was an elaborate set up preventing the FBI from hacking into the system. Adding one more layer of complication, the horse trainer lived on the premises and was always there so there was no way inside without being detected.

The only working FBI installed cameras were in the brush along the driveway and it provided a low vantage point to view the cars going in and out. They matched the owner of the vehicle to the license plates, but they didn't have much else. Most of the cars that frequented the stables belonged to laborers, and those who visited only once or twice belonged to Newport's elite interested in the horses boarded on the property. There was a white van registered to a local man who lived just outside of Providence and that van had no business being on the property. The van held at least 10 people, and the owner had no work history of any substance. He was arrested a few times for small drug charges but never served time in prison. The van, the owner and whoever traveled in the van were of interest.

***

Now that Karen and Gloria forged a solid friendship over the past few months, she could easily ask her about Heavy D's travel schedule without raising suspicion. Karen hadn't seen Gloria in a while anyway and that morning was as good a time as any to walk over for a visit. She invited James to join her and, thankfully, he agreed. It was a muggy August morning and Karen ducked into shops periodically to revel in the cool airconditioned space. The air was so thick it was as if she could push it out of the way with her hands as they walked. Their first stop was Patti Cakes for coffee. Patti looked surprised when they arrived. "Look what washed ashore, where the hell have you been for the past few days? Did you bring your man for backup?"
"I can take care of myself Patti and I don't need him for backup, how have you been?"
Patti emerged from behind the counter and gave Karen a big bear hug, then turned to James and hugged him just as tightly. Karen laughed out loud when she saw his expression. Patti barked out an order, "go sit outside and I'll bring your breakfast."

James and Karen complied and sat at their favorite table under the huge tree. They weren't quite sure what they were having for breakfast, but they were hungry, and Karen assured James he wouldn't be disappointed. After 10 minutes, Patti arrived with her hands full. An espresso for James, an iced coffee for Karen, and two interesting looking bagels were set before them. "They're stuffed! It's my latest creation, let me know what you think." James took a big bite and nodded as he chewed. "These are great Patti, I never had anything like it." Karen chomped into hers next and was instantly impressed. "You outdid yourself this time Patti, these are awesome!" Patti was thrilled because she had another winner for the bakery. If one was to meet Patti outside of her bakery, she came off as a salty dockworker a little rough around the edges, when in reality, she was a genius in the kitchen. Karen never tasted anything from Patti's store she didn't love, not just like, but love.

Patti only stayed with them for a short while then returned to the store. Karen and James enjoyed the new creations of stuffed bagels over a cup of coffee. Karen ordered a second cup before they ventured over to Gloria's store. It was a nice change having James with her this morning. He worked a lot more lately and she missed having him around during the day. In fact, she enjoyed his company so much that morning she could have sat there under the tree with him all day.

James picked up her empty cup and returned the empties to the store. He yelled back to Patti and thanked her for breakfast. She blew him a big kiss and he waved back to her. He returned to the table smiling and Karen could see Patti's charm at work. They strolled over to Worthy Endeavors where Gloria had a similar reaction and was excited to see them. Karen wasted no time with small talk, she was on a mission to get into the stables and get back to the condo. While James poked around the store to give them privacy, she jumped right in, "it's been a while since we've had any girl time Gloria. Do you ride horses by chance?"

"Yes, I ride and Devon has a bunch of horses."

"I didn't realize he was a rider, where does he keep them?"

"Sadly, he's not a rider but he has a beautiful piece of property in Portsmouth, and we can go riding any time you like. I wish I'd thought of it sooner."

"And here I was going to suggest we rent horses for a day. What a nice surprise that Devon owns a stable full. James and I have ridden together and he looks so handsome atop the horse, I'm sorry Devon doesn't ride."

"I wish he did but he appreciates the stud fees from two of his prized stallions more than he likes riding them. Let's pick a date for a ride, we'll have lunch and catch up."

James returned once they agreed on a date, and they headed back to the condo to work for the day. Karen poured over the photos from the stables obtained by the FBI camera. There wasn't much to look at but the aerial shots were fabulous. Gloria was right about one thing the property was beautiful and Karen was surprised Heavy D had a stable full of horses. Why would a city kid have horses in the first place? It's not something he grew up familiar with and horses seemed an odd choice for him unless it was all part of his attempt to fit in. The stables were far more integral in his drug business than Gloria could ever know, and Karen had a date to get inside the building.

CHAPTER FORTY-ONE

The riding date was set for Sunday morning. It was the best day of the week for Gloria to get away since most patrons attended church services until noon on Sundays. Her one and only employee was working out well, so Gloria had enough peace of mind to finally enjoy some free time away from the store. She invested a lot of time and energy into Worthy Endeavors and finally hired someone she trusted. She never needed the money because Heavy D would gladly take care of her financial needs, but Gloria preferred to take care of herself rather than be indebted to him. The store meant a lot to her as did her boat. In fact, she never sold her houseboat even though she had moved in with Devon full-time. Although she didn't know it at the time, Gloria was smart to keep the boat because she would need a place to live once Heavy D was in jail.

Sunday was a clear dry day and Karen looked forward to the long ride now that the summer humidity had lifted. She had no preconceived ideas about the Portsmouth property but when they arrived, she was admittedly bowled over. The property was set in a wooded area barely visible from the road. The 12,000 square foot clapboard stable/office was the only building on the property, and it was in pristine condition. It housed 10 horse bays on the right of the main structure, six of which were occupied by beautiful animals that were clearly well cared for. Heavy D also rented out space in the horse barn, and Karen assumed the empty bays were used for that purpose. The main building had a sizable office, a conference room, and small living quarters for the trainer. The trainer was the only person who lived on the property and when the ladies arrived, he helped them with the saddles and reins.

Gloria looked quite comfortable atop her steed as the women trotted off on their journey. The dressage riding area was outside the stable and they slowly paced around it towards the wooded paths ahead. The property wasn't massive but plenty big enough to ride for hours. Gloria provided the history behind the 18-acre property. It is a well-known piece of land in Portsmouth and Devon purchased it shortly after he bought the house. The property belonged to a former Navy Admiral and Devon intended to pass it on to his son one day.

They rode peacefully and when they approached a stream that ran through the woods, the horses waited for the reins to loosen before they bent their heads down for a much-needed drink. They were so well trained it made for an even better ride. The women made small talk most of the day and Gloria noted that she had to pick up paperwork for Devon before they returned home.

As they rode, Karen relaxed and thought about Miguel. She was in a real dilemma over attending his funeral. As a friend, of course she should attend but she was afraid to bring James to Brazil and expose him to a would-be killer lurking in the shadows. If Axel was after her, she can keep herself safe, but she couldn't watch James all the time. She wanted to quietly decline the funeral, but she was guilt ridden over the decision. Talking about it with Gloria helped her get it off her chest even though she couldn't disclose all the details. Gloria was a good sounding board and was flattered that Karen asked for advice.

They talked at length about the funeral – either attend or not. Through their conversation, Gloria believed Karen's friendship with Miguel was casual and established through Jill's relationship with him. Now that she knew more about their relationship, Gloria confidently stated Karen wasn't obligated to attend the services. Karen appreciated her feedback and hoped to convince James to forego the funeral though that wouldn't be easy. What Gloria didn't know was that James was indebted to Miguel for avenging his daughter's death and Karen was certain he wanted to attend. Gloria listened without judgment and Karen appreciated her friend's advice planning to take the matter up with James when she got home.

They worked their way back towards the stables and agreed it was a beautiful way to spend a day outside in nature away from work.

They trotted out the wooded area onto the gravel driveway and pranced right by the hidden cameras in the shrubbery. No doubt the team saw Karen as she rode by with Gloria and waited with high hopes for her report. Heavy D was a careful man, he didn't slip up and didn't leave clues lying around so Karen wasn't optimistic she would find anything significant during the visit.

Security on the property was monitored at all times. The security system was always on, the trainer lived on site, and Heavy D's men swept the office/conference room for monitoring devices every day. They were very careful. Karen hoped to fill the gaps once she got inside. Since Gloria needed to bring papers home, Karen had a chance to follow her into the office to see what it looked like.

The FBI had a detailed list of visitors to the stables. Some were employees of Heavy D but the van's coming and going seemed highly suspect for only six horses boarded on the property. There were landscaping and cleaning needs, of course, but the white van was parked for 12-16 hours per day. Knowing the van could hold 10 people made it an obvious outlier from other cars on the property. It was all the FBI had to go on for now.

After the ride, the ladies stepped inside to freshen up and Gloria remembered to pick up the papers for Devon before they left. She asked Karen to wait in the living room while she entered a code into a keypad on the wall and went into the office alone. Karen was disappointed she couldn't follow but once Gloria was inside the office, Karen wandered freely through the facility.

The nearest room was a living room equipped with a taller than average sectional leather sofa and a large screen TV. There wasn't much else in the room and she imagined Heavy D's crew waiting for him while they watched sports on the big television. The next room, a bedroom, was equipped with a twin bed, it was the trainer's room and he lived on the property. She didn't poke inside his room just in case he showed up while she looked through the house. Next was the galley kitchen. There was a huge refrigerator flanking the small cook space; it took up a full wall leaving no room for a table. Inside the fridge were all kinds of beverages, wine, champagne, and other gourmet snacks. She helped herself to a bottle of vitamin water and continued looking around. The next room was a vet's office. It had a sliding wooden doorway that was used to bring horses in for medical treatments. The room was sterile and looked like a large hospital operating room.

The entrance to the stables was just off the kitchen and there wasn't much more to the facility except for a conference room and Heavy D's office. She returned to the living room where she waited for Gloria. The room was bright and sunny in the late afternoon, and she stopped at the window taking in the view of the stunning property. From her vantage point at the window, she noticed a set of stairs behind the huge sectional. Odd that a set of stairs would be installed in the floor without a safety railing. The stairs were built to be concealed, almost like a hole in the floor. The giant couch blocked anyone from seeing the stairs and she had a hunch that she just found gold. She yelled out to Gloria, "How are you doing in there?" "Sorry Karen, I just need a few more minutes."

Knowing Gloria wasn't finished in the office, Karen descended the first few steps and stopped when she saw the small camera perched above the doorway. It pointed downward from the door jamb ready to photograph anyone on the last step. Karen found the staircase by accident; therefore, the taskforce probably wasn't aware of it either. She wished she had the time to get into that cellar, but Gloria was due from the office any minute. Karen planned to set up another riding date and next time, she would find a way to get into the basement. Gloria emerged while Karen stood at the top of the stairway.

"What are you doing over there?"

"I didn't realize there was a basement, does the trainer live down there?"

"No, the trainer has the room next door. There's nothing down there except for drugs that need to be kept under lock and key. Devon worries about a break-in from someone looking for narcotics. He keeps access to that room tightly restricted to protect the controlled substances they sometimes need for the horses. I haven't been down there."

"It's none of my business what's down there, I hope I didn't overstep?"

"Of course not, I couldn't find what I was looking for in the office and had to call Devon. I apologize for taking so long. Would you like to have a glass of wine before we leave? The refrigerator is always stocked with something nice, how about a white?"

No one entered or exited the property while Gloria and Karen sat on the front porch enjoying their wine. It was a quiet and peaceful setting, and the longer they sat in rocking chairs drinking and relaxing, the more obvious it was that the stables were the perfect cover for a drug operation. Karen didn't fall for Gloria's story about narcotics being stored in the basement, though Gloria may, or may not, know what the basement is really used for.

CHAPTER FORTY-TWO

Axel returned from Florida and was more at ease once back in Brazil in his comfortable surroundings. He was never a big fan of traveling by air. Shortly after he returned, his father showed worrisome signs of trouble. He was out late, he wasn't sleeping much, and it was obvious, he was gambling again. The debts were out of control and he needed Axel's help. He worried about the garage because he couldn't keep up with the expenses and the exorbitantly high loan payments from the local gangster. Axel was indifferent about his father's gambling problem, but never understood why he never quit after he promised him he would so many times before. He demanded an explanation of the finances behind the family business and it was in that discussion that he learned about the loan that was overdue. In the past, he came to his father aide without question but, this time he needed more information before he could fix it.

The two men discussed the garage finances for the next hour and Axel listened without judgement while his father outlined the monies due. He was indebted to a local mobster, the loan payment was overdue, and a collector was after him. The money Axel earned from Jorge could easily cover the debts and Axel promised to repay the loan shark on behalf of his father. Mr. Vascone Sr. had been in debt many times before and Axel always bailed him out of trouble, and this time was no different.

Mr. Vascone Sr., known as Fern to his friends, had a gambling problem that started a long time ago. As teenagers, a group of Fern's friends often got together to play cards and made friendly bets on the game. As they got older, the group bet on sporting events, soccer matches mostly, and since soccer was the national sport in Brazil, they could bet on just about anything related to the game. They bet against each other, on Jersey colors, first goals, number of infractions called by a referee, you name it, they bet on it. Fern bet a few dollars in the beginning, but as his confidence and winnings grew, the size of his bets grew. He won and lost thousands of dollars over the years. Besides betting on sports, he bet on horses, dogs, and even alley cock fights.

Axel didn't want the family garage to go under, so he agreed to make things right. They only had each other and Axel was a loyal son. Fern hoped to pass the garage on to Axel one day and it killed him to have to ask for money, but he had nowhere else to turn. Axel's mother died when he was a senior in High School, and after that, he fiercely protected his only remaining parent.

Axel had one condition before granting the loan; that he be the one to deliver the money. Fern agreed but warned Axel that it was dangerous to face the thugs on their turf and suggested he find a public place for the money exchange. Fern also confessed that the gangsters charged all the local business owners a "protection tax". Everyone in town paid that tax if they wanted to operate a business. Axel's anger swelled as he finally had the whole picture. It now made more sense why his father was struggling to pay everyday garage bills as there wasn't much left. Axel set out to put a stop to this immediately. Fern pleaded with his son to leave the matter be, but Axel wouldn't let anyone extort money from his family especially a gangster from the same neighborhood.

Fern eventually acquiesced and gave up. Axel had all the names of the gangsters he owed money to. For the past six months, Fern paid protection taxes to two young black men and, while they never hurt him, they intimidated the hell out of him. Axel never noticed the duo at the garage, so Fern explained the payment process. He took the money to a diner a few miles away from the garage, met the men there, and paid the monthly fee the first of every month. Fern's time slot was 8:00 am sharp, and he was never late!

The teens hung out at the diner all day collecting taxes. If a business owner missed a payment, the teens went to the establishment to collect in person. It was trouble if that happened. The business owner was severely beaten and an additional 30% was added on their already late payment. If a second payment was missed, a wife or child was tortured next. The gangsters were ruthless. Fern's concern wasn't the protection tax, it was the gambling debt of $28,000 because he never had that kind of money. He plead with Axel to pay the debt and forget about the tax, but Axel had other ideas.

Axel's plan was two-fold. First, he had to ensure no one lent his father money again or let him gamble on credit, and equally as important, the protection tax had to stop. Axel was able to protect his father better than any gangster could, and he wasn't going to pay a tax that was nothing short of extortion. The gangsters weren't protecting anyone; they lined their pockets on the backs of hard-working townsfolk. On the first of the month, Axel planned to meet the teens at the diner in his father's place. Fern gave it one more shot at convincing him to back out but it was in vain. Axel made up his mind, and he was committed to the plan.

CHAPTER FORTY-THREE

On August 31, the day before the protection was due, Axel was parked on Via Regional Road about a block up from the diner. He watched the foot traffic all day. There was no sign of the two young black men his father described anywhere near the diner, but he never doubted his father's account. Finally, at 4:00 pm two black men sauntered up to the diner and escorted the owner to his car. The men chatted by the driver's side door, and the owner handed over a small brown bag. The tallest one who wore a bandana under a baseball hat fanned through the stack of cash. After that, all three men got into their vehicles and left. Axel followed the car with the teens. They drove an old brown Camaro full of dents with an exhaust pipe that shook every time they revved the engine. With music blaring loud enough to rattle the windows, they were an easy target to follow. Axel kept a safe distance behind but remained just close enough to see the car if it turned. He followed them deep into the slums of Salvador.

Shortly after the road changed from pavement to ruddy dirt, the teens pulled into a rickety garage that appeared barely strong enough to hold up the structure above it. They emerged from the garage and ascended two flights of cement stairs built into the hill of a front yard before they arrived at the porch of the old house. The porch had a dirty couch with tattered arms, 4 folding chairs and a huge fan that was powered by an extension cord that extended through the rickety screen door. The teens handed the bag to someone in one of the folding chairs and went back down the stairs to their car without any conversation. Axel remained inside his car and watched the group on the porch. There were a few men talking and smoking but none of them appeared to be the one in charge.

Finally, a chubby older man emerged from the house grunting when he stepped through the doorway. He wore a yellowed tee shirt with black pants that looked uncomfortably tight. He made his way over to the couch and sat with a huff. The others stopped talking and it was clear that the man who just emerged from the house was the one in charge of the motley crew. His scruffy beard hadn't seen a razor in quite some time and, from the looks of his hair, he must have just woken up from a nap. A middle-aged woman emerged from the house shortly after him with a cup of coffee. She handed it to him, adjusted her hair, and descended the stairs carefully. No one paid any attention to her as she walked up the dirt road until she was out of sight the men on the porch roaring with laughter at some private joke. Axel decided he had seen enough.

He quietly got out of his vehicle and approached the cement stairs. The men on the porch stood and watched with interest as Axel walked up the three flights of stairs towards the porch. In Portuguese, they yelled out, "you've gone far enough" and Axel continued as if he never heard them. Within seconds, the casual group on the porch produced semi-automatic weapons and the laser dots from the scopes danced around Axel's torso. They yelled a second time, "what do you want?" Axel answered them but never stopped moving, "I came to discuss my father's tax." The man on the couch, told his men to put the weapons down, and signaled Axel to approach with a hand gesture.

Axel slowly made his way up the last two steps and stood before the chubby man on the couch. "Who is your father?" "Ferdinand Vascone, and the protection tax will stop now". "Is that so?" Axel grabbed the gun from the man standing closest to him and shot two men standing on the porch before they discharged their weapons. The chubby man on the couch didn't flinch as two of his men fell over the folding chairs and landed on the porch with a thud. Once shots rang out, two more men flew through the screen door and Axel held a gun an inch away from the right temple of the man on the couch. The man calmly nodded and signaled the two men to go back inside. Axel lowered the weapon to discuss business without interruption.

The chubby man was impressed by Axel's confidence and ability to handle a weapon. He asked Axel what he intended to give him if he was to let his father out of the tax payments. Axel stared at him blankly for a moment, then shot the chubby man in the head. He went inside the house to find the rest of the crew. He heard them scurry through the house and Axel hunched next to the humming refrigerator near the back door. The men whispered to each other, and Axel waited for them to find their way to the rear exit door. Axel never made a sound as the two men checked their path to the back door. They made a mad dash for the door when they thought it was safe. Axel killed them both in seconds, dropped the weapon, and stepped over their lifeless bodies.

Axel checked the rest of the house and there was no one else left inside. Now that he cleared the threats, he found the payment books and tossed them into a spare duffle bag. The protection tax was remedied, and his father was almost free from the gangsters' stronghold. The gambling debt was next, and Axel had plenty of money to use thanks to Jorge's prompt payment. He received $100,000 for the first two hits and a $10,000 bonus because he delivered Jorge's message to Miguel before he died. Axel could pay the $28,000 debt, and everyone can move on. It won't be that simple, but he can handle the aftermath.

CHAPTER FORTY-FOUR

Fern Vascone was good and drunk by the time Axel returned to the garage. He assured his father there wasn't any trouble. Of course, Fern appreciated Axel's efforts, but worried about what came next. The gangsters Axel just killed were part of the local mob and no one murdered a mobster without consequences. He worried about retaliation that was sure to follow. Fern tried a second time to dissuade Axel from getting in contact with the mob boss who ran the local gangs. He encouraged Axel to pay the debt locally instead of going to "the boss" but Axel aimed to cut the head off the snake and needed the one in charge to do that. Fern gave Axel what he needed and stayed out of the way.

While Fern worried about Axel's safety, deep down he knew Axel could take care of himself. Axel had what he needed, the name of the mob boss, Senior Marquis Torres. The Torres family lived in a modest home a few blocks away from the ocean in Salvador, Bahia, an affluent area far from the slums where Marquis Torres grew up.

Axel did reconnaissance on the Torres property before he made good on the debt. He was a careful planner and always had a backup plan to be prepared for the unexpected. Sr. Torres was a wealthy drug dealer, a member of the mafia, and a ruthless killer. His home encompassed the top corner of a block. Surprisingly, the house was not that far from the street; however, it was surrounded by a solid cement wall capped with barbed wire, and a manned iron gate across the driveway. A line of Rosewood trees partially hid the cement wall, but Axel noted the protective wire atop the wall through the trees. It was a busy road and he parked two blocks away from the house before he canvassed the property on foot. He walked around the block and got a good look at the Torres home through the driveway and entry gates. He noted two well-armed guards outside but had no idea how many guards might be inside.

Axel drew up plans as he sat in the car outside the Torres property on the side of the road. Once over the wall, he would first take out the guards who covered the yard, then enter the home undetected. He planned to systematically kill each interior guard until he had unfettered access to Sr. Torres. Once Marquis Torres was isolated, the debt will be paid, and he will ensure no one lent his father money again. Axel wasn't intent on killing Sr. Torres because a mob hit had to be sanctioned and he respected rules, but the guards inside the house were not bosses and he was free to eliminate them, if necessary. Now that he had a plan devised, he headed home to rest confident he would be seeing Marquis Torres soon.

Axel slept soundly that night until the alarm woke him at 4:00 am. He methodically went through his morning routine and arrived at the Torres home by 5:00 am, as planned. He selected a Rosewood tree just east of the Torres house and parked in front of it for cover. He climbed the tree and situated himself into a perfect vantage point while he aimed a rifle at the guards in the yard. He had a silencer on the gun but once the first shot was fired, the guards would inevitably hear something in the stillness of the morning hours. Axel eyed the guards in his scope. He counted on them not immediately recognizing the sound of the shot which gave him enough time to take out both guards before anyone inside the house was alerted. The street was empty at that early hour and Axel waited for the right moment to strike; he wouldn't pull the trigger until he knew he could take out the targets with one bullet each.

He adjusted his stance in the tree and readied himself for the first guard in the northeast section of the yard. One shot, one guard down. The other guard in the southwest corner of the yard wore headphones, and the loud music distracted him from the surroundings which made him an even easier target. Second shot, second guard down. There was an unexpected third guard in the driveway who stepped out for a cigarette break. That guard heard the gunshot and ran for cover in front of the privacy wall. He crept along the wall in the darkness never having seen where the shots came from because the suppressor took away the flash from the gun. The guard searched for the assailant without alerting anyone inside the house. Slowly, he inched away from the cement wall. His flashlight broke the darkness as the beam scanned upward into the Rosewood trees. While he searched, he stepped back just far enough into the open unaware that Axel had him in view. Third shot, third guard down.

Axel nimbly climbed down from the tree and ran back to his car. He placed the rifle in the trunk and retrieved a thick piece of leather. He ran back to the Torres house and tossed the leather over the barbed wire then quickly scaled the wall and landed on the other side. As a safety precaution, he had a small handgun hidden in his right boot. He slipped into the house ready to subdue the guards inside.

Axel slipped through the unlocked front door, found a guard half asleep in a chair in the sitting room and quietly strangled him. Once the guard stopped wriggling, Axel leaned his head back in the chair to make it look like he was still asleep. He heard someone in the kitchen preparing coffee and snuck up behind the man. Axel caught him completely off guard but felt something heavy and cold pressed into the back of his neck. He stopped dead as ordered.

A guard held Axel at gunpoint while Marquis Torres entered the kitchen wearing pajamas and a matching silk robe. The heels of Senor Torres' leather slippers clicked against the tiled kitchen floor as he met Axel face to face. "What are you doing in my home this time of morning?" Axel said nothing. "Who sent you here?"
Finally, Axel answered. "I came to see you sir, to repay a gambling debt."
"Repay a gambling debt, are you crazy? I should kill you right now for breaking into my home!"
"I wanted to speak to you personally sir, to ask for your help with a matter"
"You come into my house, kill my guards, and you want help from me?"
"Yes sir."

Sr. Torres wasn't sure if Axel was crazy, or someone he should hire to protect him. He cautiously gave Axel time to speak. The guard lowered his gun and Axel introduced himself. A guard stood nearby with his gun on Axel and never lowered the weapon until Sr. Torres was confident Axel wasn't a threat. While the two men talked, the remaining guard dragged his dead partner outside. Sr. Torres and Axel sat at the kitchen table while the elder man drank his morning coffee. Axel sat stoically until Marquis Torres asked him to speak.

Axel explained that he was there to pay a gambling debt on behalf of his father, Fern Vascone, and as he reached inside his jacket to retrieve an envelope of cash, the guard in the kitchen was instantly at his side with a gun at his temple. Axel assured everyone he was only reaching for Sr. Torres' money. He laid the envelope on the table and Sr. Torres was impressed. "That's a lot of money. I will take Sr. Vascone off my book but this doesn't make us even. You caused a lot of trouble here this morning and I want something from you now - if I decide let you live." Axel's expression didn't change, as he waited to hear the request from Sr. Torres.

Sr. Torres wanted to know who killed his crew in the slums point blank on their front porch. Axel didn't answer him and Sr. Torres grew increasingly angry by Axel's aloof attitude. He asked again and Axel answered, "I don't know who killed your crew, but I can find out under one condition. I need assurances that you will never lend my father money again." Sr. Torres laughed, "You are a crazy man to ask me for help but, for some reason, I like you. I like your confidence. You remind me of myself, and I need a man like you working for me." Axel wasn't interested in working for Sr. Torres and at that moment, he changed his mind about killing the mob boss. He crossed his leg and slowly removed the handgun from his boot. From underneath the small kitchen table, he shot the guard and turned the gun on Sr. Torres. With one final shot between the eyes, Marquis Torres fell off the chair on to the kitchen floor knocking over the coffee cup on his way down. Blood soiled the red and white striped pajamas as Axel stepped over the two lifeless bodies. He picked up the money from the table and retreated to his car. He killed a mob boss and when the organization discovered, he will be marked for death.

CHAPTER FORTY-FIVE

When an unsanctioned mob hit happened it was big news and wasn't long before Jorge caught wind of it. Sr. Torres' video surveillance clearly showed Axel inside the house, and as expected, a hit was ordered for both Vascone's. Jorge wasn't part of local mafia, but his men crossed paths with the mob gangsters often enough that both sides agreed to keep out of each other's way. Jorge had no leverage with the mob, but he needed Axel's services often enough that he summoned his driver and met Axel at the garage for another private conversation. Axel appreciated Jorge's words of warning but already assumed he was targeted. He expected an army of machine gun wielding men intent on killing them both soon. Axel assured Jorge he was ready, he appreciated the concern, but he shouldn't worry. Jorge dictated next steps in spite of Axel's confidence. He devised a plan for Fern and Axel to suddenly disappear for their own protection. Axel respected Jorge and, in the end, went along with the plan solely to protect his father.

Jorge's plan included a fiery accident where Axel and Fern appeared to have perished in a horrific way. Though he knew Fern wouldn't be happy with the plan because it meant his business was lost forever, Axel trusted that Jorge knew what was best under the circumstances and followed orders. Fern's future employment was also outlined in the plan. He would serve as Jorge's personal mechanic while he lived on the Travares estate until Axel returned from his next trip to the U.S. It was then that Axel learned Jorge had found James and Karen. The couple recently returned to Newport, and it was time for Axel to finish what he started. It was the perfect time for him to disappear while things quieted down in Salvador, and Jorge promised to protect Fern while he was away. Jorge had all the bases covered.

Axel listened intently while Jorge explained all the details of the plan. Axel was confident he could deliver while. Jorge stressed time was of the essence. Jorge readied his men to blow up the garage that night so Axel and Fern had only an hour to gather their belongings. Axel decided not to share all the fine details of the plan with his father, the less he knew the better.

Fern realized there was no turning back once he understood the enormity of the mess they were in from his gambling debts. Axel convinced him to forget about the garage and pack up personal items he wanted to keep because they were leaving, and they weren't coming back. Fern knew this would happen once Axel went after the mobsters, but he wanted to know where they were going and what the plan was. The father and son quickly discussed the next steps, but Axel left out the details about the garage being destroyed. Fern was led to believe Jorge created a diversion to get him to safety and was unaware his business was about to go up in flames in a matter of hours.

Axel and Fern were transported to Jorge's estate and settled into the guest house for their undetermined length of stay. Axel rode a borrowed motorcycle to his apartment where he retrieved money from the safe in his closet and packed a few additional items for the next trip to the U.S. He vowed to make a new life for himself and his father when he returned to Brazil. He hoped his father understood the dire circumstances they were in because of his gambling problem.

Jorge arranged a disaster at the Vascone family service station and dispatched a team to set fire to the property. Due to the gas tanks and chemicals inside the building, the explosion shook the entire city block. The Vascone property carnage was aired on the late edition of the local news. Poor Fern was horrified when he saw the footage of his family business in rubble. There was nothing left except smoldering embers of the business he worked so hard to build. Axel watched the news footage alongside his father and promised a new life when he returned from the U.S. Fern was in shock as he watched the explosion over and over again on the TV set.

There was a knock at their door, it was Jorge. Axel thanked him for his help and Jorge handed him an envelope with plane tickets, and another $5,000 in spending money. Axel quietly whispered he would kill

Karen and James for free in exchange for protecting his father, but Jorge assured Axel the terms of their deal were still in place. He would be paid in accordance with the contract once he completed the hits and his father will be safe while he was away.

CHAPTER FORTY-SIX

When Karen returned from horseback riding with Gloria, she called Mark to discuss her findings. The newly discovered basement was a hot piece of news. She promised Mark a closer look the next time she was on the property. He was particularly interested in the number of the cars they saw going on and off the property. There were peak times of traffic, sometimes 7 days a week 16 hours a day and then there were periods of little to no traffic. To be sure, the horses and grounds needed care, but that effort didn't involve enough work to keep staff busy for that long. Nor should the workload vary so dramatically day to day.

If Heavy D's employees processed drugs in the newly discovered basement, that could account for the travel patterns and so-called visitors on the property. The only door to the basement was at the bottom of the stairs in the living room and there was a camera atop the door jamb. It was impossible for Karen to come up with a reason to get through that locked door with Gloria nearby. The only logical way in there alone was to come back another time. She was hungry and put Heavy D out of her mind for the moment. There was a cookbook on her desk and she pored over it to see what peaked her interest.

James showed signs of restlessness after living in Newport for four months. The condo was beautiful and its proximity to town was nice, but it wasn't the same as their more expansive home in Florida. Karen sensed his unease and promised a home cooked meal and, even though she wasn't a great cook, James was gung-ho to help her in the kitchen. "I want to do this for you and you don't need you to help me. Why don't you go and relax and I will take care of dinner by myself" He reluctantly agreed and she decided on lemon pasta with shrimp and homemade Alfredo sauce. She may have bitten off more than she could chew on, but she wanted to show her appreciation for his patience.

She pulled the meal together in an hour and the house smelled great! James emerged from his office quite pleased with the aromas in the kitchen and saw the table set with candles and a bottle of champagne chilled in a bucket. He hugged her, "I'm looking forward to dinner - it's date night." "I'm glad you see it that way, it IS date night and I have something special planned for dessert." He raised an eyebrow and smiled coyly. They enjoyed the meal, and it was nice to eat at home rather than a restaurant with other people an ear shot away from them.

James poured the final glass of champagne and proposed a toast, "Here's to my favorite chef, would you like to go away with me for the weekend?" She was excited at his proposal, "Of course! Where are we going?" He planned a weekend away in Nantucket and had the plane ready to go first thing in the morning. They were scheduled to fly out of Providence at 9:30 am Saturday for the quick flight to Nantucket. They finished their champagne, and she lured him to the bedroom with a bowl of strawberries and whipped cream. His eyes lit up when he saw the bowl of fruit and he carried her the rest of the way to their room. He laid her on top of the bed, pushed her hair away from her face and said, "You are the most exciting woman I've ever met" and kissed her deeply. They hurried to get their clothes off and Karen almost rolled off the bed while she kicked her jeans to the floor. Their passions rose and their bodies comfortably entwined.

James daubed the whipped cream on her breasts and scooped it off ever so slowly with a strawberry. Karen followed with a dollop of whipped cream on his thigh and traced his mid-section with a strawberry until he was so aroused, he set the bowl of strawberries on the night table, and they were enwrapped in each other for a second time. As they laid together in the dimly lit bedroom, Karen rubbed her hands through his chest hair. Her mind was empty except for the delicious thoughts of their last two hours together. James hugged her tightly, "you've worn me out, but I will remember this dessert for a long time."

CHAPTER FORTY-SEVEN

They arrived at the airport by 8:00 am Saturday morning. Their last-minute vacations were exiting, and Karen looked forward to the weekend on the island. The flight from Newport to Nantucket Memorial Airport was just under an hour so they had enough time for a quick breakfast on board. They drank mimosas with their meal and before she knew it, they landed. Once through the small airport terminal, there was a car service awaiting them. James had that same look he had when he surprised her with dinner on the beach, and it felt like Christmas morning. He gave the driver the address on Washington Pond Rd and even though Karen didn't know her way around the island, the word "pond" was in the address, so they must be near the water.

When they arrived at the estate, Karen was in awe. She tried to take in the sheer size of the mansion James arranged for them.
"This place belongs to a friend of mine and it's all ours for the weekend."
"I've never seen a house this big, it's beautiful. I can't believe we have the entire place to ourselves."
"We sure do, just the two of us and few staff members."

As they approached the secluded clapboard house, it was hard to miss the sprawling front porch that wrapped around two thirds of the fabulous home. The glass front door was etched in an ocean wave pattern and the open floor plan provided a complete view of the living room, dining room and kitchen. Windows surrounded most of the first floor with breathtaking views of the ocean off in the distance and the décor was tastefully appointed.

James steered her towards one of the eight bedrooms where they found rose petals strewn across the crisp white comforter. It was beautiful and romantic. The adjacent bathroom suite was the size of another bedroom. There was a large spa tub already filled with warm water, and it was obvious that no detail was left to chance. After a long hot bath together, Karen was so relaxed she almost napped in that luscious spot. There were two robes and thick plush towels already laid out on the bathroom counter. They helped each other dry off, donned the robes and proceeded to the back patio. The island breeze was cool but not cold and she tilted her head back against James' chest. The sun warmed her face, as melted into the safety of his loving arms. They had a light snack and decided not to open the chilled bottle of white wine on the kitchen counter. Karen didn't want to drink too early because she knew James likely had other surprises up his sleeve. He spoiled her when he got the chance, and she loved every minute of it.

She toured the rest of the house and imagined furnishing a place with 8 bedrooms and 10 bathrooms. There was a sizeable art studio in the back yard behind the garage, and the property was an inspirational place. The owner was an attorney friend of James and his wife, Shelly Lampour, was a popular local artist. Gloria would have recognized her even though Karen never heard of her. The artist's works were displayed throughout the home. Ms. Lampour was very talented and very successful.

There was a chef on site for dinner and they dressed for the occasion. Karen brought a black dress with gold beaded straps and sandals to match just in case they dined some place nice. She fussed over her appearance to make sure her hair and makeup was perfect. James appreciated how she looked in sweatpants and messy hair, but she wanted to fix herself up extra special. When she arrived in the living room, he was reading the newspaper but when he saw her, he put the paper down. "Wow, you look amazing. Let me pour us a glass of wine." The chef introduced himself and announced dinner would be served at 8:00 pm. It was 6:30 pm and their first appetizer was just about ready to be served.

James started a fire, and the warmth slowly surrounded them. It was late fall and it got much colder at night. After a few sips of wine, the chef appeared with the first appetizer. They enjoyed Greek shrimp prepared with bacon and feta with all three flavors evenly represented rather than the bacon domineering the light taste of the shrimp. It was the perfect start to the evening. They moved to the dining table before their main course was presented, and Karen gazed at James in the glow of the candlelight. It was a romantic setting.

The remainder of the meal was a treat. Dinner was served over a 90-minute span during which they never had reason to leave the table. As the dinner progressed, James grew quiet; he had something on his mind. He reminisced about Elizabeth and Karen was relieved he opened up and shared his feelings with her. Surprisingly James said, "I want to start a foundation in Elizabeth's honor, and I would like you to manage it." Karen was stunned that he saw her at the helm of something so important. She had an urge to jump into his arms and say yes but she remained seated on her side of the table and responded simply, "I would be honored to."

They remained at the table talking for quite some time while they savored a chocolate dessert and two glasses of port. The foundation's mission was simple, it was set up to provide financial backing to a deserving candidate who aspired to attend law school. The sizeable scholarship and/or grant, was awarded to high school senior with good grades from lower socioeconomic areas where college was outside of their realm of possibility. James had an analyst from his office provide a preliminary assessment before he presented the idea to Karen. The statistics of college graduates who were first in their family to graduate college, and scholarship recipients from lower income areas, boasted high success rates and incomes levels. It was an interesting endeavor, there was a lot to digest, and Karen was ready to dig into to all of it.

They easily agreed on the criteria, scholarship eligible candidates must have demonstrated community involvement, or volunteer assignments in non-profits supporting those in need. Elizabeth was a tireless advocate for the underserved, and a grant recipient must have those same qualities. James endowed $10M towards the cause and already had a fund manager in place whose sole job was to manage and grow the funds. Karen imagined the lavish fundraising events and it was quite an undertaking. The Elizabeth Caulfield Scholarship Foundation was officially on the table and James promised a full-time assistant whenever she was ready. She had so many more questions but now wasn't the time; she wanted to relish in the beautiful surroundings for the night. They moved to the couch, snuggled in front of the fire and shared an espresso crème brule with local berries.

Karen relaxed into the couch while James continued the discussion about the foundation. "I started working on the skeleton of the program shortly after Elizabeth passed. I wasn't keeping it a secret from you, but I assumed I would assign the project to someone at my Company. The more I thought about it though, you kept coming to mind. I like the idea of us working together on this, and I especially like being part of a gift that changes a young person's future. I am so happy you are excited to do this."

"Oh James, I am so flattered you asked me. I'm not really sure where to begin but there isn't anything I wouldn't do for you."

They remained close on the couch until the fire dwindled to hot ashes and, when they climbed into bed, she felt closer to him than ever. The weekend couldn't have gone any better and James promised a nice long walk on the beach before they flew back to Newport.

The morning sunlight washed over the room as Karen opened her eyes while James slept peacefully for a few minutes longer. She decided not to wake him and carefully slid out of bed. She dressed and found freshly brewed coffee ready in the kitchen. The aroma filled the house. It was a little too cool to sit outside so she stood at the window in the living room and savored the coffee. She watched lively birds flit through the trees and bushes. They sang their hearts out that morning and her heart sang right along with them.

Like magic, their breakfast was laid out on the counter though it was a little eerie that someone was in the house preparing the spread while they slept. Karen never heard a thing. It amazed her that James invited her for an impromptu trip, and all of her favorite breakfast items were there in front of her on the counter. Who took care of those details for him? This wasn't the first time he surprised her with a last-minute getaway that was planned well ahead of time. Karen deduced it must be his executive assistant who did the intricate planning; she was the miracle worker behind the scenes, and she deserved a raise!

Karen watched the morning nature outside the window, until she was sadly distracted by thoughts of Axel Vascone. She hated that FBI business interfered with her peaceful thoughts that morning but the connection between Axel and the recent tragedies could not be a coincidence. It was confirmed that Axel was in Providence and Boca Raton at the same time Jill and Miguel were murdered and he flew there directly from Brazil. Who was he connected to? Karen hadn't put the pieces together yet. She heard the shower running upstairs and made a quick call to Anthony for one last favor.

"Good morning Karen, what can I do for you." As usual, Anthony was all business. "Could you let me know when/if Vascone lands on US soil?" "I'll put a tracker on him and text you." "Thanks Anthony, I owe you." After the call, she poured James a cup of coffee and brought it up to the warm and steamy bathroom. She dropped her robe and stood naked outside the glass shower doors with the coffee. James opened the glass door and invited her in. She gladly accepted, put the coffee on the counter, and he turned on the second shower head. After a long sensual cleanse, she was doubtful the coffee was still warm. As they are toweled off, James thanked her for the special delivery and the coffee was still warm enough to drink. In an extra sassy way, she replied, "happy to jump start your morning." He hugged her and they made their way downstairs for breakfast.

After their delicious morning meal, an hour walk on the beach was a perfect end to the trip. They were scheduled for a 1:00 pm departure and once again, the timing was perfect. They had plenty of time to pack up and Karen had a chance to see more of the island on the ride back to the airport. Nantucket reminded her of old New England. It was very apparent those who lived on the island had a lot of money. The homes were huge and private yachts dotted the harbor. The cobble stone streets were charming, the restaurants quaint and expensive but then, it must cost a fortune to run a business whose every supply had to be ferried over. It was a great place for a quick getaway and Karen had lots to share with the girls next time they got together.

CHAPTER FORTY-EIGHT

Karen met the girls for lunch the day after they returned from Nantucket. As usual, Patti was all ears while Karen relayed the details of their surprise getaway. Patti lived vicariously through Karen's relationship and was awestruck most of the time. Karen found it endearing and she assured Patti that she too was bowled over most of the time. No one treated her like James did. Of course, Karen didn't get into all the details but described the home they stayed in and let the girls guess the profession of the owner. They guessed a doctor first, then CEO type and Karen let them go a few more rounds until Patti tossed out "lawyer." "Yes, the owner is a corporate attorney and must make a ton of money because the house was bigger than most places on Nantucket. Presidents have also spent time at their home." Karen continued, "and there's more!" Shelly Lampour was next on the agenda and Gloria recognized her name right away. This time, it was Gloria who provided the education about Ms. Lampour. She was in fact very famous in the art world, and Karen was impressed by depth of Gloria's knowledge.

Karen also shared the news about the foundation and Patti was amazed by all of it. Patti said, "James is too good be true" and Karen nodded in agreement. Gloria chimed in, "you're so bold, that's the reason James picked you to run it. It's impressive and if there is ever anything I can do to help you, just let me know." Karen thanked her friends for their support and Patti signaled the waitress to bring them another round of wine. "We're celebrating, so it's a two-glass day today." Karen smiled appreciating the time with her friends.

Gloria was a little restless all through lunch, claiming she had too much coffee that morning, but Karen wondered if it was something more than that. She had been moved into Heavy D's house without her knowledge, and she wasn't happy about it. When their second glass of wine arrived, Gloria proposed a toast. "How about the three of us go horseback riding?" Karen jumped at the chance to get another look at the basement, "works for me, I'm in."

"Oh child, there is no temptation on earth that would get me up on a horse. Do you know how high they are off the ground? That's a long way down for this old body, I'm out."

Gloria was very sympathetic to Patti. "We aren't going to ride like cowboys and there is a trainer on the property who can help us find the right horse for you. I promise you; you'll enjoy it."

"You're a doll, but I'll pass. You two go and send me a picture, that's as close as I want to get to a horse!"

Gloria and Karen quickly compared schedules and decided on Friday; Gloria had to be in the store all weekend and that day worked for Karen. Now that the tourist season was over, Gloria's only employee was cut back to a part-time schedule and Gloria covered Saturdays by herself. Karen was somewhat disappointed Patti wasn't riding because she would have added a laugh and may have been a good distraction while she tried to get into the basement.

Karen was a little tipsy after that extra glass of wine and didn't feel much like working. She walked part of the way home with Gloria who returned to the store to work. Gloria never said much more on their walk and Karen didn't press her to talk. They were going riding soon and she'll find out what was bothering her later. They had minimal small talk while they walked, and it was almost uncomfortable. They had become good friends over the past few months but that walk felt like they were strangers. When it came time for Gloria to make a right to the store and Karen a left to go home, she asked for a quick hug. "If you need to talk, I'm here for you." Gloria was on the verge of tears, "Thanks Karen, I'm okay." They went their separate ways and Karen was left to assume Heavy D caused her strange mood.

Karen arrived back at the condo mid-afternoon and James was packing. "Where are you off to?"

"I have to be in London, do you want to go with me?"

"I wish I could, my dear, but I have a few loose ends to wrap up here."
He asked her a second time anyway. She helped him pack and picked out a few of her favorite ties.

"Isn't someone supposed to do this mundane chore of packing for you? You know, since you're a Mogul and all."

He smiled broadly, "I think the wife of a mogul is supposed to pack for him."

"HA! Now I especially don't want to get married if it means I have to do THAT." They always had such a good time together and since James was leaving around 7:30pm it left them a few hours before he had to go.

They spent the rest of the afternoon together in bed. She didn't want him to leave but never said so out loud.

"When will you be back"?

"Tops a week. I bought another Company and I need to be there for the board meeting. I have to do a little glad handing for a few days."

"You bought another company? You say it like you got a new car and I'm sorry I didn't know."

"Don't worry about it, I don't like to talk about work, it's what I do, it's not who I am."

"Okay but if you ever want to talk about it, I'm right here."

"I know you are, and I need to get in the shower, do you want to join me?"

She watched James's sedan pull away, made herself a light dinner, and turned on the TV until she was so tired, she dragged herself up the stairs to bed. She slept like a rock and spoke to Mark the next morning now that she planned a second trip to the stable. They compared notes during the call and although she had nothing new to add besides the riding date, Mark believed she was on to something big. Her return ride was well timed because the traffic on the property had increased over the past few days. Her gut told her the additional head count was in that basement processing drugs and she intended to find out if she was right.

CHAPTER FORTY-NINE

Karen met Gloria at Worthy Endeavors on Friday morning and offered to drive to the stables. Gloria had to make a bank deposit first and after that quick stop, they were off. Gloria wasn't as quiet as she was the last time they met up but she still seemed bothered. When Karen pulled up in front of the stables there were two other cars parked in the small lot. One of the vehicles belonged to the trainer, she recognized his car from the last visit, and the other vehicle was the white van that had been on the property many times before. They didn't enter the house, instead they used the outside entrance to the stable that took them directly to the horses where the trainer waited for them. Karen had to use the restroom and Gloria apologized for not asking ahead of time.

The doors were locked, and the house alarm was on even though there were extra cars outside in the lot. That was odd when people were inside the house, but Gloria didn't seem surprised by it. She unlocked the door, disarmed the alarm, and let Karen in. Karen scanned the living room as she proceeded to the bathroom, and never saw anyone else in the house. It was oddly quiet while Gloria and the trainer waited outside for her.

When Karen emerged from the bathroom, she was startled after almost bumping into a young woman who walked by her holding a beverage she just retrieved from the kitchen. She had dirty blonde hair, a small silver hoop earring in her left nostril, a faded Red Sox tee shirt, jeans and her clothing looked like she picked them up off the floor and threw them on. Karen said hello, but all she got in return was a passing "hey" without making eye contact. The young woman continued to the living room and Karen watched her from the hall as she descended the stairs. Karen waited in the hall until she heard the door open with an airlock sound, it closed, and she heard a "click" as the latch was locked from the inside. Karen never heard another sound and as much as she wanted to investigate further, she had to let it go because Gloria was waiting for her outside. Gloria had to know there were people in the basement because of the number of cars outnumbered the people on the property. Karen thought she would ask her about it once they were out of earshot of the trainer.

She proceeded outside and they were ready to ride. Karen hopped up into the saddle, but it didn't feel quite right and she walked the horse slowly around the gravel area. The trainer adjusted the foot holds until she felt more comfortable. As they rode towards the trails, Karen debated whether or not to ask Gloria about the young woman she saw in the house. She didn't want to tip off Heavy D with questions from Gloria and quickly decided against it. She will wade through the taskforce photos of student mules once she was home. If she finds a photo match to the young woman she saw today, it will prove the basement was used for drug processing. For now, it was only a hunch, and they had no concrete proof.

The two women had a great ride and once they were halfway through the day, Gloria finally confided in Karen. She admitted to being quiet lately because of problems at home. Now that Gloria and Heavy D lived together, it was not all she hoped it would be. "Devon is busy all the time and I'm not happy about what keeps him busy." Karen tried her best not to interrogate her, and instead, let her continue the conversation at her own pace. "He is a good man, and I love him, but he's not the kind of father I would have pictured for my child." Karen stopped the horse. "Are you pregnant?" "No, but I thought I was. My period was late, and I panicked rather than relish in the thought of being pregnant. I know how hard it was for Markis and I can't imagine another child born into Devon's world. We are growing apart while we are living in the same house if that makes any sense." "I'm sorry Gloria, it does make sense. I'm sorry."

They rode deep into the woods and while Karen had empathy for Gloria, she also hoped Gloria stayed with Heavy D long enough for the FBI to wrap up the case. At that moment, Karen decided definitively not to tell Gloria about the young person she saw in the house. She didn't want to stir up any more trouble for her at home and, while she cared about Gloria's feelings, she cared more about the investigation.

Karen contacted Mark the minute she returned from the ride and requested the surveillance photos to see if anyone fit the description of the young woman she saw in the hall. Mark was fairly certain he remembered a young blonde girl with a nose ring. She could be the first new lead they had in the case. He sent her the picture of the woman in question and while it wasn't a close-up photo, Karen saw the bottom half of her face under a baseball hat and it was clear enough to see the nose ring in her left nostril.

Throughout the investigation, the taskforce confirmed Heavy D had drugs transported into the country, but they hadn't found where he processed the raw material for sale until now. They had to be certain crews processed drugs in that basement before they could move in on Heavy D. Karen wanted to be the one to get proof of their activities to complete the complicated puzzle. Mark thanked her for the positive ID of the young woman and asked her again to get into that basement for confirmation. She promised to get down there although she has no idea how she would pull it off.

CHAPTER FIFTY

Now that Gloria shared her private concerns, Karen had a good reason to get both couples together for a double date. A long ride together might be good for the troubled couple to get their minds off their relationship. James would be all in with it and Karen hoped Heavy D would be up for it. Karen promptly phoned Gloria who loved the idea of a double date and promised to run it by Devon over dinner. After the call, Karen worked on a plant to get into to the basement before the next visit.

Devon had absolutely no interest in a couple's date with Karen and James. He owned horses for their stud fees and was surprised Gloria brought it up because she knew he never rode. He didn't spend time on the trails, but Gloria never realized he despised riding. The double date was a good excuse for them to get out and have some fun together, but it wasn't going to work. She retreated to Markis' room, and they played a video game to brighten her mood. He was leaving for school soon and she already felt lonely knowing she was going to be in that big house without him. It was time she talked to Devon about their relationship but before she did that, she called Karen for friendly advice.

Karen took Gloria's call while she sat at the kitchen island. Devon wasn't interested in a riding date and Gloria encouraged James and Karen to go without them. She sounded defeated and asked for advice on how to approach the talk she planned to have with Devon. The two friends discussed the best way to bring up her concerns. If she accused him of something, he will be defensive, and she won't be heard. However, if she told him how his actions made her feel, she might get her message across. Karen encouraged her to tread lightly. She hoped they stayed together long enough to finish the investigation.

Before they hung up, Gloria insisted Karen and James enjoy a day on the property together. It was already fall and winter wasn't far off so Gloria suggested they take advantage of the weather before the season ended. Karen accepted the generous offer with gratitude. James returned from London later that day and she gave him time to recoup from the long flight before she mentioned anything about the ride on Heavy D's property. Karen was certain James will be on board with a peaceful day on the riding trails and sets their date for Saturday. Gloria alerted the trainer and Karen was surprised by how easy it was to get back on the property. She looked forward to a day off the grid with James, but even more so, she looked forward to his return from London.

James arrived victoriously when he threw open the front door. Her skin warmed when she saw him, and she couldn't wipe the smile off her face. He never talked much about business except for a simple acknowledgement that a trip was a success or a waste of time, and this time it was a success! On the other hand, when James posed the same question to Karen, she rambled on for 20-30 minutes non-stop. He beamed while she shared random stories about her day, and she loved him even more for his interest. Once they landed in bed, their undeniable passion took over and they caressed and hugged most of the night. Karen woke in his arms when the sun poured in across the room.

The horseback riding date arrived; James unaware of Karen's plans to access the basement while they were on the property. She waited for an opportunity to present itself when the trainer wasn't around. It was noon when they arrived at the stables. James checked the handle on the front door just in case it was open, but it was locked. After a brief pause, the trainer shuffled to the door, and they heard the alarm keypad beep while it was disarmed. From her vantage point on the porch, Karen saw that the trainer readied two horses and they were already tied to the gate. The trainer assisted their mounts before the proceeded. Karen's stirrups required a slight adjustment, and once done, the couple quickly rode off towards the wooded trails.

It was a clear sunny day. Karen rode Kristy, a dapple gray 4-year-old mare that she had ridden before, and James was atop a mahogany bay colored gelding who looked huge next to Kristy. James was stunningly attractive on horseback, and she told him so the minute they were out of earshot of the trainer. He never blushed but sometimes Karen's compliments invoked a funny grin. They trotted through the trails and slowing when they approached the small brook. As the horses had a long drink, they debated which of the trails to follow next. Karen hadn't ever been on the property alone, and Gloria usually led the way, but the trails were well marked, and they wouldn't get lost if they stayed on the well-worn paths.

When James and Karen finally returned to the stable in the late afternoon, there wasn't a car on the property except for theirs and the trainers. It was so quiet and, being late in the day, there was a chill in the air. After Karen climbed out of the saddle and jumped down from Kristy, she screamed out in pain and fell to the ground. James ran to her side and the trainer emerged from the house concerned. She tried to get up but couldn't put any weight on her right ankle. The trainer instructed her to stay on the ground while he tried to help. He held her leg and she winced as he slowly pulled her boot off. James was concerned and she winked at him while on the ground. He looked confused because he didn't know if she really hurt herself or if she winked to let him know she was fine.

James scooped her up off the ground and carried her inside the house. The trainer followed right behind them after quickly securing the horses to the gate. He retrieved an ice pack from the medical room and instructed her to ice her ankle while she kept it up on the arm of the couch. She promised not to move, and James offered to stay with her while the trainer put the horses back in the stable. She assured him it was fine, only a sprain, and asked James to help the trainer secure the horses. They were Gloria's guests, and the least James could do was help the trainer. She insisted he leave her alone and James finally agreed. Both men left her on the couch while James convinced the trainer he was going to help him. The saddles had to be removed and stowed, and the horses need to be bathed before being put back into their stalls. The trainer didn't need his help, but James took Kristy's reins and started to remove the saddle anyway.

The minute the men were outside, Karen leaped off the couch. The trainer had disarmed the alarm system when they arrived, and she hoped against all odds that the camera on the basement door was part of that same system. She peered over the couch to see the camera and the small glowing light above it showed red. It wasn't clear if red meant armed, or if red meant it was off. This was her one and only chance to take a shot at the basement and she raced down the stairs. She removed a lockset case from her jacket, and it took a little longer than she anticipated to pick the lock on the cellar door, but she got the door open. Once unlocked, she carefully moved the door to open it just a crack. Her heart thumped loudly in her ears. She waited for an alarm to wail the minute she opened the door and to her utter relief, nothing happened. She quickly opened the door and slipped in.

She stood in a small area equipped with wall hooks and storage bins. The light switch was to the left of the door opening found only after she groped along the walls with her hands. When the overhead LED lights popped on, the enormous room lit up instantly. She scanned the room quickly and made mental notes of the contents. There were 4 long metal tables, at least 10 feet in length, with two scales per table, and some kind of electrical bag sealer appliance plugged into the floor. The room looked like an operating room because it was so clean and sterile. There were two drains in the floor and four hoses connected to multiple spigots coming out of the wall.

James and the trainer were due to return any minute; therefore, she exited the basement and noted that the door locked automatically behind her. Karen hopped over the back of the couch and replaced the ice pack on to her ankle. She finally had the missing piece of the puzzle as adrenaline raced through her veins. It was now confirmed that the basement had one use, and it was for processing cocaine. She finally had the missing piece to the puzzle.

James had the same look of concern when he entered the living room. Karen was there waiting on the couch, "don't worry, I'm already feeling better, I think it was just a funny landing and it may not even be sprained. The ice helped and I'm sorry I worried everyone over what looks like nothing."

The trainer insisted Karen take the ice bag with her when they left, and she barely limped back to the car. As they pulled away, Karen confessed that she didn't hurt herself. James was relieved and said, "was I supposed to react differently to your fake injury?"
"No! You were the perfect concerned boyfriend and it was just what I needed."
"Did you find what you were looking for?"
"Thanks to your help; I had enough time to get what I needed."

"Great, let's celebrate a job well done then! Uncle Tony's?"

They opted to dine inside, and the waiter showed them to a table with an ocean view. It was a perfect end to a successful day. The stable really was the perfect cover, she thought, as she popped tortellini into her mouth and sipped the delicious red wine. They agreed to send Devon and Gloria a bottle of wine as a thank you gift and James made a call to his assistant before they left. His long-time assistant Bridgette was the "other" woman in his life. She was a magician and planner extraordinaire. Karen was the recipient of Bridgette's planning efforts more than once and she was thankful James had someone so capable working for him. Between Bridgette and Kevin, he was always well supported.

The next day before breakfast, James had an early conference call in his office, a perfect time for Karen to relay the latest findings to Mark. Her phone rang just after she poured her first cup of coffee. She recognized the number, it was Anthony, and he didn't have good news. Axel Vascone was on the move. He landed at New York's JFK that morning and he was scheduled for a flight to Providence arriving at 2:20 pm.

Before Karen even fully digested the news about Axel, she had Mark on the line. "As promised, I got inside the basement. It's a sterile room with long metal tables and triple beam scales. It looked like it was washed down after each use. There was a drain in the floor and hoses were mounted on the cement wall. It also smelled like the area was recently bleached."

"Excellent job Karen, the next time we see carloads of workers on the property, we will pay them a visit with a search warrant. Did you find any drug paraphernalia?"

"I didn't find anything like that, but if you saw what I saw, you wouldn't need a second look because the purpose of that room was undeniable."

CHAPTER FIFTY-ONE

Karen hated withholding information from James but with Axel in route, she was on high alert. She told James a little white lie when she claimed she met the girls for another lunch when, in reality, she waited for Axel at the airport instead. It was the first time she was able to see him in person providing she could pick him out of the crowd. His image was burned into her brain so she was fairly certain she would recognize him when she saw him. She arrived well before his flight at 1:30 pm and found a good vantage point inside the terminal. Thankfully, the airport was small, and it only took about 5 minutes to get from the parking lot to baggage claim. All flights at the small airport exited the same way, through baggage claim. Passengers descended down two small escalators, with a staircase in the middle, or a handicapped elevator that flowed into the open area whether they had bags or not, it was the only way out of the terminal.

She stood next to a cement column hidden from Axel's view as made his way down into baggage claim. She patiently watched all the happy travelers greet loved ones until the flight from JFK finally arrived. There was a lull in passenger traffic in between flights and when the JFK passengers began filling the area, she saw Axel Vascone for the first time. He wasn't a standout in the crowd, but she recognized him instantly. He wore a baseball cap, jeans and a long-sleeved shirt. A pair of sunglasses hung from the pocket of his shirt, and he carried a small duffle bag over his shoulder. He looked to be in his early 30's as best she could tell from the distance. She remained close to the column while she watched his every move.

Axel proceeded through the baggage claim area in an unhurried but purposeful manner. He followed foot traffic into the men's restroom while she waited at the column for him to reemerge. Who was this guy and more important, why was he here? After a few minutes, her adrenaline pumped steadily as she waited for him to emerge from the men's room. A heavy-set man entered the men's room just before Axel and that man just reemerged. Maybe Axel occupied one of the stalls and he needed a few more minutes. Karen was ready to jump out of her skin with anticipation.

The clock on the wall was synched with her watch and the time lapse meant Axel was in the men's room for at least 15 minutes. After 20 minutes, he still hadn't emerged. The remaining passengers descended into baggage claim, and the crowd moved to the corresponding conveyor that held their luggage. Axel was nowhere to be found. Karen never took her eyes off the men's room door, but it was obvious, she lost him. She scanned baggage claim one more time and scrutinized all the rental car desks. Axel wasn't there, nor was he to be anywhere in the terminal. She walked around the small airport no longer worried about concealing herself and she was dumbfounded she lost him! He had disappeared, like a puff of smoke.

Axel entered the men's room, tossed the baseball cap into the trash, changed his jacket and T-shirt and put the sunglasses atop his head. He exited the men's room with a small boy in tow looking like a doting father. He recognized Karen as she stood near the column and eluded her fairly easily. He proceeded to the parking lot and picked up a car Jorge arranged for him. It was exactly where he expected it would be in the third row of short-term parking. He opened the trunk and found a rifle and ammunition. As promised, Jorge took care of all the details before Axel left Brazil, and Axel had everything he needed to fulfill his contractual obligation. He drove towards Newport with the widows rolled down and breathed in the fresh air. It was a short 30-minute drive into town.

CHAPTER FIFTY-TWO

Karen took the long way home from the airport and drove aimlessly all over town searching for Axel. She rode down the narrow side streets but after wasting almost two hours, she gave up and returned to the condo. She parked in their numbered space at the Vanderbilt frustrated that she lost him. When she got out of the car, she carefully scanned the surroundings to see if anything was out of place. She would continue looking over her shoulder until she found Axel and learned why he was in Newport. She also was not leaving James' side. There were no coincidences with Axel's travel schedules to the U.S. When Miguel and Jill were killed, he was in town and the one responsible for their deaths. She knew he was after her and James. She snapped out of her foul mood as neared the condo. When she stepped up on to their porch, James was outside reading the Wall Street Journal.

"What are you doing outside?"
"We won't have many more days like this, and I thought I would wait for you out here. I hope you had a good lunch with the girls, how about a glass of wine on this beautiful day?"
"That sounds great, I will bring out a bottle and two glasses."

James preferred to stay home rather than walk into town for a drink and Karen was relieved. Axel was lurking somewhere nearby, and they were safer there. She retrieved a bottle of Pinot Noir, two glasses and pulled together a few snacks since it was close to dinnertime. Everything on the tray teetered while she walked to the porch but thankfully, she didn't knock over a wine glass on her way out. James poured the wine and dug right into the cheese. Karen's stomach growled and she hoped James didn't hear it because she was supposed to have been out to lunch with the girls all afternoon.

It was a beautiful September day; the weather was warm with only a slight breeze. The summer tourists were gone, and Newport was more like home without all the extra buzz. The afternoon sun warmed her cheeks, but a few uninvited seagulls ruined their peaceful setting. The gulls closed in on them and squawked for some crackers. There were two sizeable gulls on the railing, and one was brave enough to hop down on to the porch. James flew out of his seat to scare the bird away and at that very moment, a bullet whizzed by them, and the condo window shattered into pieces. Shards of glass flew everywhere, and Karen instinctively pushed James to the ground. They were momentarily stunned and laid flat on the wooden porch in disbelief. Karen pushed James back into the house safely.

"Stay low, get inside, and DON'T stand up even if it means we have to crawl."
Thankfully, James listened, and they made their way inside. "Stay here, and don't go near a window." She grabbed a gun out of her purse. "Karen don't go out there!!"
"I'll be back, wait here, and call the police." She raced to the front door, cocking the gun to be sure there was a bullet in the chamber. She was ready to use it if she had to.

She slowly opened the door and kept low as she landed back out on the porch. She guessed where the shot came from and looked east down the docks to see if anyone was out there. None of the boats swayed in the water, it was quiet, almost too quiet. She checked west and there wasn't a sole around. She carefully made her way down to the docks towards the water and stayed covered. All of a sudden, she heard a crack and pain seared down her left thigh. It was as if someone stuck a hot poker into her leg, pushed on it and twisted it inside her thigh. She fell onto the dock but never screamed despite the searing pain.

While it was a faint sound, Karen heard a motor that whirred nearby. She had to find a safe place to hide but she couldn't walk. There was a small fishing boat just up ahead and she crawled towards the boat. She tried to move quickly. Sweat beaded on her forehead, she breathed heavily as she pulled herself up to the railing and limped her way over to the small boat. She dragged her left leg along the way and had to get herself on board somehow. All the while, the motor whirred in the background and as the boat drew closer.

She flopped into the small boat and grit her teeth from the pain as she rolled in for cover. She listened for the sound of the motor and perched herself in position to take aim the minute the boat and its driver came into view. It had to be Axel. She was ready for him when he showed himself. He was not getting another shot at her or any of her loved ones ever again. The police sirens wailed as they neared. She wanted to get Axel alone before the police found him to find out who sent him. Finally, she saw his image dotted through a line of boats one row away. He slowly motored along a row of bigger boats concealed from sight. Other than the low murmur of the small horsepower motor on the back of his boat, it was eerily quiet on the docks.

Karen found a small cooler on the fishing boat and rested it on the front seat for balance while she held a vigilant stance. She waited anxiously for Axel to show himself. The pain in her leg subsided enough that she concentrated on her mission. She had one focus and that was protecting James from this mad man. The police spread out on the docks, and she heard their radios crackling in the background. Axel hid behind a large yacht out of sight, but Karen heard the small motor idle.

She carefully scanned every boat in the row across from her, but it was difficult to get a clear view. The sun was setting, and she had to find him before darkness set in. The police scattered around the docks both east and west, but Karen never yelled out her whereabouts. Something moved on a large yacht, and she focused on the image in the steering house. Was that a person? As she watched the figure intently, it moved; someone was up there. Axel found her hiding place from the higher vantage point in the steering house.

He quietly jumped off the boat onto the dock and ran towards Karen darting in and out behind columns. He wore sneakers and didn't make a sound, but she saw him running and ducking. She readied herself to take the first shot and the police emerged. "Stop, police, drop your weapon." Axel stopped in place and boldly stood in the open with a gun pointed right at Karen. She rolled over on to the floor of the boat no longer able to see anyone and gunfire erupted on the docks. As soon as she fell out of sight, Axel turned towards the police and fired. The officer closest to Axel was shot in the neck and dropped instantly. He then turned his gaze right and took out the second officer with one more shot to the head.

The remaining two officers radioed for backup and alerted the dispatcher that two officers were down. They continued firing at Axel but neither hit him. Karen carefully lifted her head to see if Axel was still in the same spot hidden behind a column. She didn't have a clear shot. The remaining two police officers yelled for Axel to drop his weapon, but he didn't listen. Instead, Axel aimed at the third office just as a hail of bullets rained down on him. Axel fell to the dock and the gunfight was over.

Karen held herself up long enough to confirm Axel was hit. Chaos erupted as other officers fanned the dock. Through the noise, flashing lights, and impending darkness, she saw the most comforting sight. James was on the dock and she cried out to him. She tried to sit up as he ran towards her. He grabbed the small boat, pulled it closer and leapt aboard. While he hollered at the top of his lungs for the police, he held her tightly.

James rode with her in the ambulance to the hospital. Karen needed surgery to remove the bullet and James stayed with her until they separated in the hall outside the surgery room. After three hours, the surgeon emerged and announced that Karen will make a full recovery. She woke up in the recovery room and found Detective Chuck Workman next to her bed. Karen had nothing to tell him and didn't know why anyone would want to harm her. Detective Workman sent the bullet they removed from her leg to the lab to see if it was a match to any other murders in the area. He was determined to find out why someone would be after her or James. He asked Karen if she and Jill were involved in anything together that would cause someone to come after them. He proposed that Jill's unsolved murder was tied to the shooting on the docks and Karen had nothing to add. While she knew it was the same person, she can't help the detective or James would be in danger. She also had too many skeletons in the closet that might be exposed if the detective snooped into Axel's life in Brazil.

Chuck Workman continued questioning her, but Karen was too tired to stay awake and drifted off to sleep. James asked the Detective to leave her alone and let her rest. He promised to cooperate once Karen was back on her feet. The Detective agreed to leave but promised to return again soon. James never left her side until he was certain she had enough strength to get out of bed. Karen hated anyone fussing over her as she tried her best to let James care for her.

After a day and half in the hospital, Karen was allowed to return home. James hired a nurse, and though Karen scoffed at the idea initially, she was so appreciative of his efforts, she let the nurse help out. Once home, she was propped up on pillows on the couch while the nurse took her blood pressure and temperature. The nurse readied the guest room, but Karen insisted she was fine now that she was settled in at home and it was not necessary for the nurse to be there 24 hours a day. James had different ideas and insisted she spend the night and that was the end of the conversation.

The surgeon's instructions were straight forward. Crutches for the next few days while she shuffled around at home, then a cane as tolerated. She was advised to get off the couch every hour or so and to keep blood circulating properly. She was determined to use the cane as soon as possible to hasten her recovery. While she laid on the couch rehashing the last 24 hours, she was thankful for those seagulls on the porch. She began sobbing and gasped for breath through her tears. James heard her and raced into the room.
"What's wrong, are you in pain?"
"No, I was thinking about those seagulls, if you didn't jump to scare them away when you did, I could have lost you." She shook from sobbing so hard.
"I'm fine and you're going to be fine, that's all that matters." He laid next to her on the couch and held her head in his hand until she stopped crying. She drifted off to sleep on his chest and he carried her to bed. She was soundly asleep and never woke while he got her settled.

The next day, she felt much better, and Chuck Workman was due at 11:00 am. She was not all interested in more questions from the Detective and went over his head. Karen called the Police Commissioner's office directly and made it known to the assistant on the phone that she had information about the recent shootings on the docks. The commissioner came on the line after only a brief hold. Karen identified herself as a Consultant with the FBI and requested a meeting. Her information was too important to share over the phone and even more important, she didn't want to converse on a recorded line. The

Commissioner agreed to meet her at his office as soon as she could get there.

The Police Commissioner held the door as she made her way into the office on crutches. Her leg was killing her, but she wanted Detective Workman off her back, and this was the best way to do it. The Detective ultimately worked for the Commissioner and if he called Workman off the case, that ended any further questions. First, Karen explained her role with the FBI. While she was no longer an agent, they asked her to support the Taskforce on a drug case. As a former agent, she had many enemies and, though she didn't know who the shooter was, she can't disclose the details of the ongoing investigation, but she believed it was connected. She offered condolences for the officers who were killed, and she offered Mark's contact number at the taskforce office if the Commissioner wanted to speak to her boss directly. Detective Workman needed to back off, and Karen had nothing further to say to him. The Commissioner thanked her for coming down and Karen was confident he wouldn't call Mark because the local police and the Boston FBI field office teams barely cooperated with each other.

Before Karen left the Commissioners' office, she was privy to his call to the Chief of Detectives. He specifically asked the Chief to remove Workman from the shooting because it was handed over to the Feds. She was little unsteady as she walked to the car. James tried to help her but she insisted on getting there by herself.

Once in the car, Karen confessed Axel's identity to James.
"I owe you an apology. Axel Vascone is the name of the man the police killed on the docks."
"How do you know that? Is he part of the FBI case?"
"No, he is from Brazil. I think he killed Jill and Miguel, but I can't prove it. I can't tell the police his name or I'll have to explain who he is. I kept it quiet to protect us. I'm sorry I didn't tell you sooner, but I wasn't certain he was after me, nor am I yet 100% certain he came here to hurt us even though it sure looks that way."
"I'm disappointed you didn't tell me sooner, but now that he's dead I hope that's the last time we have to talk about Brazil."

CHAPTER FIFTY-THREE

Upon returning home, Karen hobbled to her office and called Mark. She dreaded telling him she was shot and, to no surprise, he was shocked to hear the news. She provided a plausible story and told him there was a mad man on the docks. They were drinking wine on the porch one minute and the next minute someone opened fire at them. It was a random incident. Mark offered help in an investigation, and she assured him there wasn't anything to investigate since the shooter was dead and she never heard of him. "Karen, this may be a good time for you to leave Newport and recuperate back in Florida. We are getting ready to move in on Devon Smith, and it would be better if you weren't with Gloria during the raid."

"I thought you needed more evidence? I've been working on another visit to the stables."

"No need, we are ready. One of our men inside in the body shop in NC confirmed that drugs are being processed and packaged at the stable just as we suspected. We finally had enough to get a warrant. Between your work, Jason Andrews's information and the latest from the body shop, our years of work culminated in an arrest warrant!"

Karen was overjoyed to hear Heavy D was finally getting what he deserved and the thought of recovering in the Florida sun sounded perfect. Her leg was healing but still really sore. She clapped one hand on her desk feeling a huge sense of accomplishment.

She had a hint of melancholy for Gloria and Markis, but it was short lived knowing they have each other whether Heavy D was in the picture or not and Gloria wouldn't leave Markis alone without a father. She never got a specific time or date but the raid at the stable was set to happen later in the week. The next time the white van was at the stable, they would move in. Heavy D will be arrested simultaneously at home. The student in custody, Jason Andrews had been instrumental. He helped the task force understand the overseas component, gave the agents a full account of his drug activities, and provided step by step instruction he was given to carry drugs back safely from Columbia. Thankfully, Jason was in protective custody until the trial.

James waited for Karen to emerge from the office. When she opened the door, he was a few feet away in the hall. They stared at each other with fondness until she broke the silence. "How about we get back to Florida so I can start building the Elizabeth Caulfield Scholarship Foundation?" James' heart just skipped a beat. "I can't think of a better idea, when would you like to leave?" "I'd like to say goodbye to the girls, how about one more day?" "Consider it done."

Karen made a small list of the items she wanted to keep from the condo and Bridgette made arrangements to send those items to their home in Florida. The only personal items that really mattered were the Wallingford's and James agreed. Otherwise, the Newport condo felt more like an office than a home despite it being nestled in a beautiful seaside town. When James offered to get take-out from Uncle Tony's, she appreciated the short walk to the kitchen versus the long walk to town on crutches. The plans were set to meet the girls for lunch the next day to say goodbye and she hobbled over to the table.

James drove Karen over to Patti's for the final lunch under their favorite tree. She made her way to their table long before the girls arrived. The crutches were retired and now she used a cane but left it leaning against a railing. Gloria arrives first and gave Karen a big hug. Patti wasn't far behind and immediately squawked about the shooter on the docks. Neither Patti nor Gloria knew she was shot during that commotion and Karen never told them what really happened.

"Did you hear about the mad man in the news, two police officers were shot and killed, and the gunman was shot right over there" as she pointed towards the general direction of the docks. Gloria chimed in, "What is the world coming to?"

"We heard the gunfire and the police sirens from our condo. I actually hurt my leg in all the commotion. I slipped on the kitchen floor when I ran toward the window and ended up with this nasty bruise."

"You poor thing, that's what you get for having such a clean kitchen floor." Patti was a perfect comic relief to change the subject.

"Ladies, I have some news…. now that winter is coming, we are going back to Florida. My work wrapped a few weeks ago and we are ready to get back home. I'm surprised we stayed this long." Gloria teared up but, surprisingly, Patti was completely understanding.

"You have been a delightful friend. Will we see you next summer when you want to escape the humidity in Florida?"

"I hope so, I would love to see you both again." They chatted for a bit longer until Karen had to go. Patti gave Karen another hug and whispered that she will be missed. Gloria sat with Karen until James arrived. She appreciated their friendship, thanked Karen for the advice and promised to keep in touch. Karen wished her the best with Devon and Markis, the women hugged, and Karen drove off with James.

CHAPTER FIFTY-FOUR

James surprised Karen after lunch. There was a limo in the parking lot at the condo and, once James parked, a well-dressed driver assisted Karen out of the car and into the back seat of the limousine. James arranged a drive to Connecticut to visit her father's grave site before they returned to Florida. She was so touched by his kindness. In fact, it was the nicest thing anyone had ever done for her and exactly what she hoped to do before leaving. Now that Heavy D was going to jail it made visiting her father's grave that much sweeter.

It was a forty-five-minute drive to the cemetery in New London, Connecticut. When the limo pulled in, the driver knew exactly where the headstone was located. Karen was again touched by Bridgette's thoughtfulness. Before Karen was halfway out of the car, James rushed to her side to help. She wanted to walk to her father's grave site unassisted and he understood.

James held her steady once in front of the headstone, "your Dad is proud of you, just as I'm proud of you." She had been to her father's gravesite many times before but this time a tear rolled down her cheek. She stared at the stone and told him she helped arrest his killer, but she didn't say the words aloud. As the limo slowly drove out of the cemetery, Karen took one more look at the headstone through the window. Finally, her dear father could rest in peace. She did it all for him and it was over. They had a quiet ride back to Newport and found their bags all packed by the time they returned. She was eager to get back home and equally eager to receive confirmation that Heavy D was in jail.

During their flight to Florida, Karen and James split a bottle of wine. While they relaxed, the FBI and DEA raided Heavy D's stables and found six people processing cocaine in the basement. Another team descended on Devon Smith's home, and he was arrested quietly in the presence of his lawyer. Thankfully Markis had returned to school and never saw his father taken out in handcuffs. While being escorted out of the house by police, Devon assured Gloria it was all a misunderstanding, and he would be back by the end of the day. However, she knew better and packed her belongings. It was time to return to her houseboat. She waited to hear from Devon or his attorney from there.

There were 37 arrests made in conjunction with the case, that included airport employees, dock workers, body shop technicians and TSA agents but most important, the missing student Karen fretted over was safe. Rebecca Jones was found in a Cartagena prison and the Feds promised to get her back to the US safely. Mark phoned Karen once everyone was in custody and thanked her for her help. She was, in turn, grateful to him for reaching out to her to work on the case. She helped put her father's killer behind bars, and there was immense satisfaction in that.

She watched the news every night until she saw the broadcast she had waited for. While lying in bed she saw "him", Devon Smith, aka Heavy D, on the TV screen. She stared at his mug shot. James paused the TV and asked her to stay put. She heard the "pop" of a champagne cork and he returned to the bedroom with two glasses in hand. They returned to the newscast and enjoyed the champagne. It was the perfect time for a celebration!

They toasted each other while they listened to the array of people arrested in connection with the case. It was a live segment, and the FBI was about to make a statement. The taskforce leader was asked to come to the podium. Mark adjusted the microphone and thanked the agents assigned to the taskforce and those in the field for their tireless efforts. Karen talked to the TV screen, "you're welcome Mark". She giggled nervously because, despite her contentment, she felt a tiny seed of discomfort and insecurity still smoldered. Who hired Axel Vascone to come after them? However, happiness triumphed over angst as she remained in the moment. James refilled her champagne flute before they toasted their future together.

Lightning Source UK Ltd.
Milton Keynes UK
UKHW052006220223
417146UK00002BA/5/J